Among Friends

Among Friends

Caroline B. Cooney

BANTAM BOOKS
TORONTO · NEW YORK · LONDON · SYDNEY · AUCKLAND

AMONG FRIENDS

A Bantam Book / November 1987

The Starfire logo is a registered trademark of Bantam Books, Inc.
Registered in U.S. Patent and Trademark Office and elsewhere.

All rights reserved.
Copyright © 1987 by Caroline B. Cooney.
Book design by Judy Stagnitto
This book may not be reproduced in whole or in part, by
mimeograph or any other means, without permission.
For information address: Bantam Books, Inc.

Library of Congress Cataloging-in-Publication Data

Cooney, Caroline B.
    Among friends.

    Summary: Six high school juniors discover surprising,
often painful, things about themselves and their relation-
ships with the people around them in the diaries they
are asked to keep as a three-month English assignment.
    [1. Self-perception—Fiction.   2. Friendship—Fiction.
3. Interpersonal relations—Fiction   4. High schools—
Fiction.   5. Schools—Fiction]   I. Title.
PZ7.C7834Am   1987   [Fic]   87-18853
ISBN 0-553-05446-5

Published simultaneously in the United States and Canada

Bantam Books are published by Bantam Books, Inc. Its trademark, consist-
ing of the words "Bantam Books" and the portrayal of a rooster, is
Registered in U.S. Patent and Trademark Office and in other countries.
Marca Registrada. Bantam Books, Inc., 666 Fifth Avenue, New York, New
York 10103.

PRINTED IN THE UNITED STATES OF AMERICA

FG   0   9   8   7   6   5   4   3   2   1

For my son, Harold

December

Emily's diary

Everybody who had Miss MacBeth for English last year warned us that The Assignment was coming up, but still we thought we could bring Miss MacBeth around. We'll read an extra Shakespeare play, we promised, we'll read *Moby Dick,* we'll read *War and Peace,* we'll read any book with 800 pages, but please, please, please don't make us keep diaries!

Miss MacBeth just passed out spiral notebooks with green pages, like the ones secretaries use for shorthand. "You'll find these easy to fill," she said.

There are sixteen of us in advanced junior English. Sixteen moans rose up like a chorus of dogs at the pound.

"*Fill?*" we said, horrified. "Miss MacBeth, you expect us to *fill* these books? What are we going to *say?*"

"Whatever comes to mind," said Miss MacBeth. "We'll keep them for three months. You'll be surprised at what happens in your lives over three months." She smiled, but her smile landed, of course, on Jennie.

I looked at Jennie too, but I didn't smile.

Once there was an Awesome Threesome.

Jennie and Hillary and me.

You come across a lot of best friends, but we were the

only trio in school history. If only The Awesome Three-some still existed! Jennie would first of all talk Miss Mac-Beth around and get us a better assignment. Teachers try to please Jennie, instead of the other way around. And if Jennie lost, and we did have to keep diaries, Jennie would make it such fun! We'd read each other's entries, and laugh around the clock. Or else Jennie would think up some crazy diary-writing technique to make everybody else in the room wish they could be part of The Awesome Threesome, too.

Today was like old times for a minute. Jennie and Hillary and I stood there in the hall after English class staring at our blank notebooks, leaning against each other to make a tepee: Jennie always said three made a perfect support.

Like third grade. I still remember the day Jennie said we were going to learn to jump rope or die trying. She made us stand in the road with that piece of clothesline all day, and we even missed lunch; we lied to our mothers and said we'd eaten at each other's houses. But by the time it was dark, we could each jump into the rope and do any pattern we'd ever seen done.

Today we straightened up from the tepee and Jennie said, "Let's play 'This Hallway Is Ours.' "

She invented that game on the first day of high school, when we were scrawny little ninth graders and everybody else was lost in the maze of halls or struggling to remember new locker combinations. We were scared of the seniors because they seemed so old and sophisticated, so tall and well dressed. But we linked arms, because Jennie said that if we'd been The Awesome Threesome in junior high, we'd *really* be The Awesome Threesome in high school. We marched down those unfamiliar halls like the

Salvation Army taking over a street corner, and even the seniors got out of our way.

We haven't done that in ages.

For a while I thought the change in The Awesome Threesome was from summer. After all, I had a job at McDonald's and Hillary's grandmother took her to Europe and Jennie—I don't even know what Jennie did all summer. It was the first time The Awesome Threesome went separate ways. And somehow it's not going back together. Or rather, Hill and I go together, but Jennie—Jennie's "busy." That's Jennie's word for when she's being a success and we're just going shopping.

Sometimes before class, we find that I've studied two hours a day all week for the test—and Jennie forgot about it. But I'll get an 83 and Jennie will get 96 without trying.

When I've wept over my hair, I go to school and see Jennie all fluffy and sparkly, and I know that the most she's ever done is run a brush through her hair once.

When you're little kids, jumping rope together, you don't know you're going to be dull. You think you're going to be exciting and popular and gaudy and bright. And Jennie *is*!

Whereas I'm just Emily.

Jennie is racing on ahead; her speed in life is twice mine. I'm slogging along back here, choking on her dust.

I'm jealous.

Terrible, terrible word.

Jealousy is a little ball inside me, like a malignant tumor. As long as it stays a little ball, I'll be okay, I can control it. But what if the ball bursts? What if it spreads through me like some dreadful stain?

I can't tell my mother, who would be ashamed of me. I can't tell Hillary, because she doesn't seem to have bad feelings toward Jennie. I can't tell Jennie, because it's not Jennie's fault she's terrrific and I'm ordinary.

Look at that. I even put three "r" 's in terrific. Jennie's terrrific deserves more than the usual number.

All autumn this jealousy has been building. Now I'm choking on it.

So I guess I'm lucky to have a diary. Somebody to tell.

Oh, how weird! I'm calling the diary *somebody*, as if it's a person who understands, not a bunch of wired-together green pages!

Hillary Lang, her journal

I don't know about this. A person could be sorry she wrote things down. I like Miss MacBeth, and I like her assignments, although sometimes it tires me out that no matter how clever I am, Jennie is cleverer. Miss MacBeth has this huge piece of purple paper on the board and in the center of it she puts the week's best composition of any of her classes. I swear I am not exaggerating when I say that Jennie Quint has been there every single week for two years. A person should know when to back off. Jennie only knows when to surge on ahead.

In physics, of course, she's the one with the laser experiment that makes all the rest of us look like third graders learning the four tables.

In English, of course, she's written some fabulous short story, which is now up on the purple paper.

In German, of course, she sits next to Paul Classified and they flirt in foreign languages.

And now we hear from the Drama/Music Department that the Christmas production is an original pageant, music, costumes, and choreography by Miss Jennie Dunstan Quint.

I can't stand it.

And the worst thing of all is, her complexion is always perfect. That girl has never known what it is to face the mirror in the morning and see yet another horrid spot bursting out on the tip of her nose.

Miss MacBeth gave us her solemn promise that these diaries would be guarded with her life and nobody else would read them and they would not be posted or excerpted from. Miss MacBeth, I don't know whether to have faith in you or not.

I wonder what these journals will accomplish. Paul has so many secrets we could probably auction off his journal at the end of three months and pay for our whole junior prom. But I know Paul; he won't give away a thing. Probably record the daily temperature instead of his thoughts. I still have my crush on Paul Classified. It's funny how tantalizing he is just *because* he never responds! I think Paul Classified is so good-looking. Paul has a silent presence. You're always aware of him: strong, tall, unbelievably quiet. Paul doesn't fidget, or tap pencils. He doesn't adjust his jacket or tell jokes. Before he talks there's a slight pause: Paul planning ahead so that each sentence will reveal as little as possible. I want Paul Classified to love me.

Jennie's all bright-eyed and starry about something. At first I thought it was Paul Classified, but no. "Oh, it's this project I'm doing," she said vaguely, as if I wouldn't be able to understand the project.

7

Jennie and Emily and I were little girls again during passing period. It was fun, and it worked, just like it used to, but it doesn't fit anymore. The Awesome Threesome. That used to be the pivot of my entire life: the trio of us. It's different now. I still want to be friends, but I don't want to be The Awesome Threesome.

I'm sick of Awesome.

I want Jennie to be ordinary again.

Paul's diary

You transfer into another high school and people are curious. They know your name; the teacher puts it on the blackboard. But you're anonymous in blue jeans and sweater. So they ask questions, as in, "Hi, Paul. I'm Jennie. Where are you from?"

Okay, she's Jennie. Cute, sparkly. But I'm not going to tell anybody anything. They learn one thing, they're going to want to know another. I've practiced my new smile in front of the mirror, and it's a good one, stretches my lips back, and everything. I say to Jennie, "I move a lot."

Right off, from the first day, I mean to stay away from Jennie, because she's the type who will win: if she wants to know me bad enough, eventually she will. But I stay around her because she's exciting. She's my first genius. I might never meet another one.

In physics lab Jennie is assigned to be my partner.

Jennie flirts like mad, and I start liking her, but I keep a grip on myself.

Jennie says, "What do your parents do for a living that they have to move so often?"

The whole lab is listening, so I say pleasantly, "Oh, this and that. They blow hot and cold on lots of stuff."

Next time we have lab Jennie says, "Paul R. Smith? That's your name? My middle name is Dunstan. What does 'R' stand for?"

Again the whole lab is listening. Even the teacher. I manage to smile. I say, "Why should it stand for anything?"

Jennie laughs. She asks another question and it's one I can't answer with a crafty little quip. I wipe the grin off my face and pay attention to the lab. Jennie's getting a little close for comfort. Things are bad for me and I can't risk it.

Funny: I've moved four times and it takes months to find your slot and make friends. This time I swear off friends and overnight I've got status. I'm popular because I'm a mystery.

One day we're filling out forms that request your middle name. "Oh, good! At least we can find out one thing about Paul," cries Ansley. "His middle name!"

I can't stand Ansley. First of all, that's not a real name. Second, you can't tell from the name she's a girl. Third, Ansley is preppy. I don't like preppy. Reminds me of my—

No.

This may be a journal, but that doesn't mean I have to reveal any secrets.

The teacher looks at my paper. I've written the letter "R" where it says middle name. "So, Paul?" he teases. "Even your middle name is classified information, huh?"

Instantly The Awesome Threesome starts calling me

Paul Classified. The nickname circulates through the entire high school in like six minutes flat. The gym teacher, the kid with the locker next to me, the freshmen in my woodworking class, everybody in English—they're all calling me Paul Classified.

At first I was going to put up a fight.

Then I think, it's like armor. Whenever they get a little too close—Jennie is always a fraction too close, it's her nature, I guess, closeness—I can say, "Classified," and they laugh.

Jennie is part of The Awesome Threesome. I don't know if I've ever come across *three* best friends before. Jennie is the plainest of the bunch when she's quiet: average height, weight, coloring. But Jennie is hardly ever quiet. She's got enough sparkle to dim new-fallen snow on a sunny morning. Hillary is the prettiest: strawberry blond hair, green eyes, great legs. The third is Emily, with thin black hair, big soft dark eyes, and a back-of-the-room sort of personality.

Don't notice me! her posture says.

I wish *my* posture said that. People in this school notice me no matter what.

The Awesome Threesome likes to flirt with me. "Okay, Paul. So you won't go out with one girl. Go out with three instead. Want to go skiing with us in Vermont this weekend? Don't worry, Hill's mother is chaperoning."

"Thanks," I tell them. "My family has plans."

That happens to be the truth. We always have plans. Not plans I like, but plans I can't do much about.

Just before sixth period, I'm going down the hallway, focusing on physics, which doesn't come as easily to me as it does to Jennie (not that I'd tell her that) and The Awesome Threesome appears at the far end of the corridor. They have braided their hair together: Jennie's brown,

Hillary's red, and Emily's black, into one fat tricolor braid, and Emily's got the braid in her fist. The Awesome Threesome staggers down the middle of the hallway, six legs under one head of hair, taking up so much room everybody has to flatten against the walls to let them by. First Ansley, who's thin as a bookmark anyway, and couldn't get any flatter if you stuck her under a truck. Then her boyfriend Jared, who is so preppy I'm always surprised when he talks—up till then I've figured he's a store window mannequin for ski togs. Then our history teacher, Miss Marcello, who probably weighs the same as the QE II, with a prow equally large. Miss Marcello can suck in her lungs all year, and she's not going to get flat against the wall. The Awesome Threesome is laughing like crazy, their laughs braiding together like their hair: Jennie's all breath, Em's a high giggle, Hill's a deep chuckle.

Jennie winks at me. I try to stop myself, but I wink back.

I can't help it.

Her wink is all mine, all special.

And then I slip by fast.

If Jennie touches me, I'm gone, and I can't afford it.

Ansley's diary

I, Ansley Augusta Morgan, begin my journal in the autumn of my junior year at Westerly High. I would prefer to be at Choate Rosemary Hall or Miss Porter's, like my friends, but my parents believe that the public school system is good for me. They are mistaken.

Look at the retards with whom I am forced to share the halls.

Jennie and her little buddies sashayed down the halls hanging onto each other's hair, staggering like drunks attached at the roots, pushing everybody out of their way. Naturally they seized this chance to flirt with Paul Classified.

Everybody thinks Paul is so fascinating. Trust me. The only fascinating thing about Paul is that he has managed to convince the school he *is* fascinating. Underneath all that so-called mystery there's just another jock with nothing to say.

And I swear every girl in this school has a crush on him, just the way every boy gets a crush on Jennie. It drives me *crazy* when all a person does is stand there showing off—and other people fall in love with them.

Thank goodness for Jared. Another seven weeks and Jared and I will have been officially going together for one year. A January anniversary. I'll call it our Janiversary. Jared has been saying for weeks now that this winter he's going camping in the mountains in the snow. I'm going to call his bluff and get him equipment for it.

After school Mother and Aunt Isabelle and I went to Lord & Taylor's to get a few things for winter. Mother would like to ski in Italy this year. Jared wants me to stay at his family's condo in Colorado instead. At least whatever clothes I buy will be right for either one. I'm so glad that bright rich colors are in this season; I look my best in strong colors.

JARED'S DIARY

For purposes of organization, each day will be divided into categories.

1. Car: Another week, I'll have ten thousand miles on it. Remember to phone for mechanical check. First really cold day this year—heater works well. Funny jokes on morning radio.

2. School: Physics dull, lunch disgusting, English this assignment, Spanish B plus in quiz, did lay-ups all gym period, I hate basketball.

3. Girls: Ansley wore her new outfit, which looked exactly the same as what she wore yesterday, but luckily I didn't say that. Ansley always looks good to me. Jennie, too. Jennie was being crazy in the halls again today— lurching around with her old Awesome Threesome like they were still in the third grade. At first I thought they were showing off for Paul Smith, who annoys me, but Jennie gave me her special grin when they passed me. She's got a way of making you feel like God when she smiles at you. There are guys in this school who work hard to get one of Jennie's smiles and she doesn't even know.

The girls all know it, though. And boy, do they keep track of who has a crush on Jennie now! If I want Ansley to stay my girlfriend, Rule Number One is—don't refer to Jennie.

Jennie has written a musical; they were talking about

it in the band room. The drummers were working on a percussion duet she wrote just for them. Think they don't worship her! Miss Clinton, the band director, has been helping her. Miss Clinton said, "You know, in eleven years of teaching I've never had a Jennie. It's just plain exciting to be around her."

My mother thinks that one day we will point across the street and tell people that Jennie Quint grew up there, and they will gasp and say, "*You know Jennie Quint?!?*"

Unwise to say this to Ansley.

Very, *very* unwise to say this to Emily or Hillary.

4. Home: Dad's still in Los Angeles. Mom's still waiting for the construction crew to begin the addition.

5. Weather: Autumn turning fast to winter: high winds, trees bare, the yard men took the last of the leaves while I was at school.

Jennie's diary

A diary.

Scary. I don't want to do it. Once it's on paper, it's public. As long as your thoughts are hidden inside, you're okay. But diaries—Miss MacBeth is going to read them. A lot of assignments I don't feel like doing, but I've never had an assignment before that makes me want to run. The thoughts I'm having now are bad ones. I can't even think them, let alone write them! . . . And yet . . . I have this intense desire to write the best diary of all.

I like to be good.

Wrong.

I like to be terrific.

Wrong.

I *have* to be terrific.

And *that's* wrong. I can feel that I am going to pay. Some awful price is waiting for me, like a monster in the dark.

JARED'S DIARY

Just for the hell of it, I followed Paul R. Smith home today. I used to think it was funny how he won't tell anybody anything, up to and including his real name, but it's getting next to me. Especially the way every girl in Westerly High is falling under his spell. Most of the guys don't tease him—I guess it helps to weigh in at 170 and be built like a wrestler.

Coach asked Paul why he doesn't go out for sports, because they could really use him. Paul said he was needed at home. That kind of answer stops a teacher short. Says nothing, closes subject. You've got to admire Paul. He's got this technique down.

Wendy thinks Paul might have a parent in prison, and doesn't want to admit it. Keith thinks Paul's family might be in drugs—either selling or using. Hillary Lang thinks anybody named Paul Smith is definitely a fake, and the mother and father are in the CIA. Or else, in *another country's* secret service, here under false passports! Now, I ask you—is this ridiculous or what?

We were talking about it in the locker room, and Billy Torello says he heard that Paul is just very poor and has all these little brothers and sisters he has to go home to after school and take care of, like Abe Lincoln or something. I didn't remember Abe Lincoln having a lot of little brothers and sisters, and Billy Torello punched me and said that wasn't the point. So now I have a cracked rib all because Paul Classified won't tell anybody why he goes straight home every day.

One thing. He's not too poor to have his own car. He doesn't take the school bus. After all, it would have to stop near his house, and that would give things away. We might—oh, gasp!—find out something about him.

So I followed him.

I think I have a lot to learn about the undercover business.

First, I probably shouldn't be driving a new red Porsche. Conspicuous, you know?

Anyway, Paul R. Smith spotted me, waved, parked in a municipal lot and strolled into the department store. The guy's crafty. Tomorrow in English, I can't exactly say, "Listen, I was following you, and you outfoxed me; give me another chance today, huh?" Anyway, it's always possible his mother made him stop to buy towels, right?

Categories, forgot my categories.

School: No change.

Family: No change.

Car: Too red.

Weather: Who cares?

Paul's diary

Thank God for school. Seven hours a day of freedom.
Bet I'm the only kid writing *that* in my journal.

She's worse.

They fired her.

I don't blame them.

I would never have hired her to start with.

She's sort of stuck between the bedroom and the kitchen. She wanders back and forth trying to think of something to do, someplace to be.

Aaaaah, change the subject. You think about this all day, don't put it in the diary, too.

I have physics and English with The Awesome Threesome, but only Jennie is in German with me. I signed up for German figuring the only questions would be grammar and vocabulary. Wrong. I didn't know there would be a Jennie in the class. A Jennie who can ask me about my past and my present just as easily in one language as another.

Today in German I tease Jennie. "You really think you can learn something without Hill and Em?"

That trio has been together since all three of them went to the finest nursery school. Learned to ski and play soccer, learned piano and jazz dancing, learned pottery and diving and Chinese cookery.

Jennie's always ready for a chance to flirt. "Guess you'll just have to help me," she says, and all of her is teasing me: her eyes, her smile, her shoulders twisted toward me. "Every night, Paul Classified. Without fail. My place or yours?" Jennie laughs. She has this terrific laugh, very airy, using up so much breath that afterwards she gasps to fill her lungs again. I always have this crazy desire to hold her up when she laughs so her lungs won't collapse.

I never do.

One thing might lead to another.

For sure, we can't study at my place.

"Come on," I tell her, looking at her earrings instead of her eyes: she's wearing tiny delicate gold hearts. "You learn by osmosis. You just look at the page and it's part of you."

Jennie is incredibly smart. I don't mean your ordinary high marks, good tests kind of smart. I mean genius smart.

People like to be near her brilliance. As if the glitter of her star might shower on them.

Emily and Hillary are just there for the ride. They don't know that. I'm not sure Jennie knows that. One day they'll wake up and find that the Awesome Threesome has only one awesome member, and what happens then?

The Awesome Threesome is a little civilization all its own. There are girls who would sell their souls to be part of The Awesome Threesome. But there aren't any vacancies. Jennie told me that in seventh grade she and Hill and Em used to be really cruel to girls who tagged after them. "We were crude, too," she said. "It makes me quiver to think of us now. You know what we used to say to those girls?"

"No. What?"

"Here comes toilet paper, wiping up the rear."

It was so mean you had to laugh. "At least you know you've outgrown being mean, Jennie," I said.

In a queer frightened voice, Jennie said, "I don't know that." She looked at me so intensely, with those brown eyes that focus so much harder than other people's, and see so much more. "Paul?" she whispered. "Are you ever afraid of what you are?" As if she could see into a future she didn't want.

"Not to worry," I said, which was a joke. Worry is my profession.

Another time, she showed me a notebook full of ideas for a musical she wants to write: book, lyrics, music, costumes—the whole works. I felt as if I were reading an English lit. assignment, it was so professional. "Jennie, you're going places, aren't you?" I said, leafing through the notebook.

"Yes, I'm going places." Jennie fastened her eyes on me till I looked back, hypnotized. Softly, analyzing me, waiting for answers, she breathed. "But you've already been places, haven't you, Paul Classified?"

I'm on an iceberg, where the edge breaks off and falls into the sea. The ice will crash and float away—but I, I will drown.

If I had just one problem, I could face it. But there are so many, and they hurt so much that I have to turn my back on them.

So I abandon Jennie. I don't even answer her. Rude— and yet I can get away with it, because they all call it "mysterious" instead.

So I go home and pick up the pieces nobody else wants and apply a little more glue that never holds.

19

Ansley's diary

Today I know I am a very fortunate person. I have all that I want. I am rich and thin and beautiful and I have Jared. I am also the only happy person in this auditorium.

I'm taking a risk, writing my journal in the dark during the dress rehearsal, but there's so much happening and I want to get it all down. The auditorium is not yet dark. A dozen teachers, half as many parents, perhaps twenty kids are sprinkled among the five hundred seats. Jennie stands in front of the pit orchestra tapping the baton against the palm of her hand. If she is nervous, you can't tell. Jennie has incredible poise.

A head peers between the curtains. "Another five, Jennie," calls the stage manager. "We have two more kings to dress."

Jennie nods. She turns slowly, like a model on a runway showing off to the audience, sets her baton on the rim of her music stand and walks around the rows of seats toward Emily and Hillary. Everybody is watching. Jared and I are sitting in the row behind Em and Hill, and Paul Classified is about five seats to Jared's right. Emily and Hill are doing their algebra. They know perfectly well Jennie is about to join them, but they don't look up.

"I always wonder what sex they are, don't you?" says Hillary.

"What *sex* they are?" Emily is laughing. She and Hill

have dressed alike: deep blue turtlenecks under huge white sweaters, tons of jewelry, immense earrings. Hill's red hair gleams and she looks excellent, but it's too much for Em, you can hardly even see her. I'd love to take Emily shopping. Here, Emily, I'd say sternly, stop wearing yellow, stop wearing blue, throw that jewelry away and cut your hair. You have potential, but who ever wanted *potential?* A person should look good right now.

Anyway, Hill and Em are leaning so close their noses are almost touching, doing their math on the same clipboard with the same calculator. If Jennie wants to sit down, she'll have to ask permission.

The Awesome Threesome. The only known trio in high school history. Rapidly becoming a duet.

"Yeah, you know. Just why are A and B driving separately to Chicago?" says Hillary, waving her algebra problems in the air. She and Emily click pencils like swords. They don't move an inch apart to let Jennie in. "If they're both boys," Hillary goes on, "then maybe it's a car race and they've got a bet on who finishes first. But if they're both girls, the whole thing is impossible. Girls would drive together, talking the whole way. It wouldn't matter whether A or B got there first because girls wouldn't care."

Jennie, the outsider. Boy, that must be a new experience for her. I mutter this to Jared and he mutters back, "Don't gloat." Jared and I kiss in the dark. Jared is wearing a jacket and tie and looks like a future Wall Street wizard. I don't tell him I love him, I've been saying that too much lately and it's his turn. But I decide that for our Janiversary I'll get him a shirt that uses cufflinks instead of winter camping junk. If you're preppy, you should go all the way and really prep their socks off, right?

"But if A is a boy," Hillary says darkly, "and B is a

21

girl, then I want to know what went wrong between them."

Emily is giggling. I've always liked Emily's giggle. It's one of her redeeming features. "It's probably A's fault," said Emily. "He was rotten and rude and she won't associate with him any more."

"Then I demand to know why they are headed for Chicago," says Hillary. "I see no reason to continue with this algebra assignment until I have all the facts."

It's funny; we're all laughing. But it's horrible, too, because it's a little skit they've made up in order to keep Jennie out. For the first time in our lives I see Jennie scared. Jennie Quint, afraid? And of her two best friends? Nice way to launch a Christmas pageant.

"So, Jennie, what is the answer to this algebra problem?" says Emily. Math is Jennie's only weakness. Now, when Jennie is shining like a star in the east, her best friends are going to throw her only failure at her.

Jared gets involved. "Now, now, girls. Forty-five minutes since school ended, five minutes before her own dress rehearsal, and you think Jennie's had time to do her algebra?"

See why I like Jared? He's not strong on emotion, but he can be a nice guy if he wants. (Yeah, and who's he being nice to? Jennie Quint, of course. Would he step in for anybody else?)

Paul Classified says softly, "Break a leg, Jennie."

We're all startled. Paul Classified doesn't usually talk unless pressure is applied. But of course, we're talking Jennie here. A person forgets that Jennie Quint is the exception to every rule.

Jennie tells Miss Clinton she wants to sit in the audience and watch this time instead of directing herself. So it's Miss Clinton who lifts the baton, and nobody thinks anything of it—except us; *we* know Jennie is trying to make friends with her friends. Some task.

Slowly, oh so slowly, the first king leads the procession, his gift held high in front of him. His robe of midnight velvet is flecked with silver, and the second king wears crimson satin and glittering brocade.

"Jennie!" I gasp. "Those kings are stupendous! Where on earth did you rent those costumes?"

"I didn't." Jennie is bursting with pride. "I designed them this summer and I just finished sewing them last week." I am mega-impressed. New York, get ready. Jennie Quint is coming to fashion.

"In your spare time, I suppose?" Emily says resentfully.

"We don't even need a star in the sky for this pageant," mutters Hill.

"You're right," says Emily. "We could just hang Jennie here in the east and let her blaze."

Jared is laughing. "We get two plays for the price of one," he whispers in my ear. I'm sort of enjoying it too, but I'm feeling sorry for Jennie. I mean, a person usually has a team she can count on to root for her. Jennie's team just walked.

"Uh. Wait just a minute here," says Emily. "Jennie, a fourth king just came on stage."

Jennie nods.

"And a fifth king!" cries Hill. "Jennie! Don't you know that—"

"No," says Jennie. "I looked it up. Matthew doesn't tell how many wise men there were. He just says there were three gifts. I guess people have always decided there was one king per gift." A person should never argue with Jennie Quint. Jennie always has more facts than the rest of us.

"So how many kings do you have?" says Hill.

"Seven."

Emily and Hillary roll their eyes at each other. "Trust Jennie to do something to excess," says Hill.

"Honestly, those costumes," mutters Emily. "I'd have to take ten years of sewing classes, rip out each seam twice and still my costumes would look like old sheets. Why seven?"

"I had so much fabric. Plus this way there's such a great selection of kings. We've got our black king, our Laotian King, our Swedish king, our—"

"Three of your kings are queens," observes Paul Classified, his voice soft in the darkness.

And all seven, like Jennie, are breathtaking.

The orchestra plays a march cold and frightening, full of power and splendor.

I tremble, forgetting the so-called Awesome Threesome.

The kings draw near the stable and now the music becomes fragile. We will break just listening. Jennie, drawn by her own music, takes the baton after all. The music slides into a lullaby that moves us all to tears.

Jennie, Jennie, how do you do it?

Paul's diary

Christmas means presents.
Listing, buying, wrapping, giving.
My mother is not going to make it.
Scarlet stockings and a tree, twinkling lights and

24

letters to Santa? History. This year I'll get her a box of Kleenex and we'll listen to carols on the radio.

I wonder if I'll hear from Dad.

Does he think about us?

And Candy, does she think at all, let alone about us? Does she know that Mom hurts so much it's going to kill her?

I am sitting in this auditorium for the peace of it, the quiet, hoping the pageant will make me feel better. And it does. I don't know if it's the idea of Christmas, or the sound of Jennie's music, or just not going straight home. But I could sit here for hours in the dark, not thinking.

Jennie is like a candle; she lights a room all by herself. Listen to Jennie's music. Stare at Jennie's costumes.

I touch the cuff of my wool shirt, and the frayed wrist of the only sweater I have left that fits me. When everybody else was abandoning ship, I was busy growing four inches.

Seven kings.

I wish Jennie had asked me to be a king. In those clothes, you would feel like somebody.

What have I written here?

Nothing I could ever pass in.

I'll have to keep two journals. Like laundering money. Keeping two sets of books. One for Miss MacBeth, one for me.

Jennie's diary

Who could have guessed that at the moment The Awesome Threesome ended, there would also be three truly awesome kings on the stage?

My wrist was lifted to bring in the saxophones, my eyes fixed on the drummers who would join after six bars. But my soul watched my best friends, leaving without a word.

The hand that held the baton trembled.

Mary sang the lullaby I worked on all of August. Sad, sad music, because Mary knew her baby was born to die in agony.

When I composed the lullaby, I was only guessing. Now I've tasted it.

Agony is being alone: agony is the death of a friendship.

I was actually crying when the lullaby finished. The first violin, a nice boy whose only friendship appears to be with his instrument, touched me with the bow. "Good music," he said softly. "You aren't the only one crying."

I don't want some violin player to poke me with his bow! I want Hillary and Emily! I want them to be celebrating with me. Weeping with me. But to the violinist, I said, "Thank you."

(I should learn to be silent, like Paul Classified. Then Em and Hill wouldn't be mad at me.)

How little I share with Hill and Emily now!

They don't know how lyrics come: in the night, with a jolt that wakes me up gasping. I have a booklight with batteries that I pull under the covers with me, and write in the tent of my sheets: my rhyming dictionary on one side and my stage notes on the other. I get cramps in my elbows from leaning so long on them.

They don't know how the music comes either: rushing in my skull: fierce, pounding, demanding to be played. How I have to stumble away from other things—class or supper—find the piano and quick, quick, play it out loud, get it out from behind the barrier of my bones, past my fingers and onto the keys. The relief of hearing the chords the way I heard them in my head, and then the frantic effort to write them on staff paper before they're lost.

Emily and Hill don't know about Paul Classified, either.

A crush on Paul Classified is mandatory for junior girls, but I don't do the things everyone else does and they would not expect me to have a crush on Paul. But I do, and it's strong, and it rules more of my life than even music, or my parents. I have written six love songs. I turned one into the shepherds' ballad for the Christ Child, but it was really for Paul Classified. The other ones are tucked away in my music notebooks. I've never used his name, although "Paul" rhymes with a thousand words and dances in my head all the day long.

(So many secrets. I will not die of disease, but of the weight of my secrets.)

I conducted the pageant while Emily and Hillary walked away.

The star in the eastern sky lowered.

My star isn't going to come softly.

My star won't creep across a quiet sky.

It'll come with a crash.

Truth hits you. Truth isn't a chorus or a carol. If you ever understand at all, it will be to a drum roll.

The pageant ended.

My pageant.

My drum roll.

And the audience sighed, all together, as if their lungs were one.

And they stood up to applaud.

The stage crew, the light crew, the costume crew, the teacher advisers. The orchestra, Miss Clinton, who taught me how to orchestrate, Mr. Grant, who helped with the lyrics—they gave me a standing ovation.

Beauty.

Not a star in the sky nor a babe in the manger. Beauty is applause.

"Awesome," whispered someone.

Awesome: a slang word for anything from a peanut-butter-and-jelly sandwich to the Grand Canyon.

But this pageant was mine and it really and truly was awesome.

Oh, applause, applause! Is it sick, to adore applause so much? To love so dearly being the center of attention?

It stopped. It rang in my ears, carrying me, but the ringing faded, the applause was over.

The infant's hay was stuffed back into the manger. The saxophones went back into their cases. The costumes went into the drama room closets. And quickly, oh so quickly, everybody was gone. Gone to other things: supper, home-work, girlfriends, home.

The auditorium was empty.

I was alone.

Applause takes a crowd. And joy—joy takes a friend.

I want to be Awesome! I want to be the Awesomest of all!

But I don't want to be awesome alone.

Hillary Lang, her journal

I never even knew she was making those costumes.

She had to go into New York for that material. There's no fabric shop around here that would carry that stuff.

Jennie—going into the city without us?

Jennie—finding those kings, rehearsing that sax trio, without us?

Jennie—never phoning to say, "Come look at what I'm sewing"?

Emily and I just abandoned the dress rehearsal. We walked slowly to the parking lot. I'm the one with a car. Emily's not quite sixteen yet and Jennie's mother will never let her have a car, because having to drive Jennie places means Mrs. Quint can be in on all Jennie's action. If Jennie gets a car, Mrs. Quint stays home. I don't like Mrs. Quint.

I had never driven off without Jennie before. Abandoned her without a ride. It was unthinkable.

"Give me a break," said Emily. "There's no such thing as Jennie being stranded. Her personality wouldn't allow it."

"The way Paul was looking at her, he won't allow it either," I said.

Every girl in school cherishes a daydream that one

day Paul Classified will start dating and it will be with her. All mysteries of Paul will be known to one girl, but she'll keep those secrets, and become mysterious herself. And that, too—that, too, Jennie would have.

"She wrote the music and designed those costumes over the summer," I said finally. "I was in Europe, you were working. That's why we didn't know about it."

"Hillary. It's *December*. She could have tossed it into the conversation *sometime* in all these weeks."

We got into my car and drove away. I didn't feel like adding up all the weeks we three had been sliding apart.

"Do you think that Jennie—" I began.

"Don't let's talk about Jennie," said Emily fiercely. "I feel like her satellite. She isn't even here and we can't have a conversation without her."

We drove under the Christmas decorations strung across the main streets, past the windows glittering with Christmas gifts, Christmas lights, and Christmas colors. The radio played Christmas carols. "I'm even jealous of Christmas," cried Emily suddenly. "Jennie gets Christmas. I have to pretend it isn't here and that I don't care and I never wanted it anyhow."

I never think of Em being Jewish any more than she ever thinks of me being Christian, because it has nothing to do with anything. I stared at her. She burst out, "I want January, when there's nothing Jewish and nothing Christian and nobody talks about anything except skiing."

"Oh, Emily," I said desperately, "none of that matters."

"It matters terribly. I—" She broke off with a queer little gasp, and I thought, this is Jennie again. Every time Jennie is involved, Emily and I get hurt.

Winter Friday afternoons my mother packs the station wagon and we head for Vermont. The Awesome Threesome always goes to Killington. "Only a few more weeks 'til skiing weather," I said. "Maybe we should give Jennie another chance. Maybe it's only this pageant. Maybe we have a bad attitude. Maybe in January . . ."

I got on the highway, drove two exits and got off. Drove seven miles north into the country, where Lost Pond Lane creeps up the crest of a rocky hillside, and the houses look past immense oaks and thick glossy rhododendrons down into the lost pond where deer and foxes wander over the frozen marsh. Each house is unique— architect designed, featured in important magazines. Important people don't live there anymore: just rich ones.

Jennie's house was first (of course) and we drove past the Quints' and up two more to Em's. Emily gathered her junk. Emily is always burdened by objects: her purse is huge and bulging and her book bag, torn at the seams from the weight of her books, overflows. Sometimes she carries a second bag, too. What a contrast to Jennie. Jennie takes a tiny purse that holds precisely one short comb, one teensy make-up kit, a single Kleenex, a single aspirin, one pencil, one pen, and a miniature change holder into which she stuffs lunch money. Jennie knows she can handle any catastrophe that comes up, whereas Emily worries so much she has to carry her whole life-support system with her.

How come Jennie can't be ordinary? Sometimes I yearn for Jennie almost passionately—the way we were; the trio of us, silly, giggly, ordinary little girls who—

But Jennie will never be ordinary again. And no matter how hard Emily and I work, we will never catch up to her.

"You watch," said Emily. "Come New Year's Eve, we'll have yet another all-girls slumber party and Jennie will go into New York for some fabulous evening with Paul Classified."

31

"A person like that deserves to be shot," I agreed.

Emily managed to get out of the car without dropping anything, and none of the seams of the book bag ripped as she staggered in her door. Our idea of success—getting home without collapse.

Emily's diary

The whole pageant had a strange breathless quality to it.

It was us down in the auditorium trying to control our jealousy.

I took my eyes off Jennie's spectacle on stage and closed my ears to Jennie's music floating through the dark room. I studied Paul Classified's profile. The semi-darkness suited him: it was the real Paul. He's not good-looking. It's his mysterious aura that's so attractive. Like Jennie. Jennie isn't beautiful; it's her brilliance and poise that draw admirers to her: people who would perform for her, work for her, literally sing for their suppers if Jennie Quint asked them to do it.

Paul was watching Jennie.

It's not enough Jennie has the whole school at her feet. Now she's going to have Paul.

Paul's worn the same shirt and sweater for days now. I have this overpowering desire to buy him a new shirt. I have even chosen the shirt: chamois cloth, one of those beautiful dark teal shirts we saw in the Ski Shoppe. I keep dreaming of using a tape measure for an excuse to get close to him. He'd probably ask Jennie if I measured right.

When Jennie returned to the podium she directed the orchestra as if she had held the baton from infancy, the way other babies hold pacifiers.

If the kings in their velvet were soaked with sweat, I was soaked with jealousy.

Jennie is really a medium sort of person to look at. Medium tall, medium weight, medium brown hair, medium brown eyes, medium everything! And yet she sparkles, she glows, she isn't medium at all! She is spectacular! How can that be?

Our three families moved onto Lost Pond Lane within a few years of each other, and all the photographs of birthdays and excursions in my albums include Jennie and Hill. But you didn't know, when you were learning to skate backward or reading out loud the first sexy passages you ever came upon in a book—you didn't know you were going to be ordinary.

There is nothing ordinary about Jennie. Nothing. Ever.

And me—I'm like a rug. Wall-to-wall dull, blends in anywhere.

A lot of things this junior year have hurt me. I thought I would date boys. I even thought I would date Paul Classified. I thought high grades would come more easily to me and I'd have more poise. But none of it has come true for me, and all of it has come true for Jennie.

Jennie's music changed. Shepherds lifted their crooks and were progressing toward the stable. Instead of the thin reedy oboe you usually hear for shepherds, Jennie had chosen three saxophones. The music was wild and jazzy. The auditorium pulsed with the rhythm of finding the babe.

It was so good. And sitting there, being mean to Jennie, I admitted something to myself—I had been hoping her music would be lousy.

Ansley's diary

Went shopping at Lord & Taylor's. Nothing, absolutely nothing. Went to Bloomingdale's, to four boutiques, to the Ski Shoppe. Nothing.

Shopping is my favorite activity but I get sick of looking. I like to buy.

Miss MacBeth had us fill out a questionnaire about our journals.

Here is the first question:

In writing your diary, do you write down

1. intimate thoughts
2. a chronology of what happened during your day
3. description of weather and news headlines

Nobody wanted to fill out the questionnaire.

Already the diaries are too private to talk about!

Emily put her hand over her diary to keep it hidden. So now I know she carries it with her. I carry mine, too. You can't tell if Jennie Quint carries her diary—she has so many notebooks, you know: the musical she's writing, the play she's writing. Then—along with everybody else in the class—I glanced at Paul Classified. We all want to know what Paul's writing down. I'm putting my money on the weather. In my opinion he's a room-temperature personality.

Paul's diary

She phoned. I couldn't believe she could talk in such an ordinary voice. Like an ordinary person. She even sounds the way she dresses: classic preppy. I can see the collar of her white oxford shirt peeking up under her lovely sweater, and the single gold chain proclaiming her success.

Less than a year ago she destroyed my mother just by walking up to the door, as if she'd tossed a grenade through the window, and here she can call up and want to chat as if we were old buddies.

After a while I hung up the phone. It was in the middle of one of her sentences. I didn't slam it down, it just sort of fell back out of my fingers.

Mom knew who it was. She looked at the phone as if expecting *her* to crawl out of it. Mom never talks about *her*. Only about Candy.

As if Candy disappeared by herself.

Mom stood by the phone, shivering—you would have thought that we were standing outside in the sleet—but she had already cranked the furnace up to seventy—and what happens when the oil bill comes? What then? "But I tucked Candy in," whispered Mom. "I read Candy bedtime stories. I pushed her on the swing. I baked cookies with her."

I tried to comfort Mom, but the thing is, I don't know how to comfort somebody. All I can do is stand there. I ice up, even with Mom. What are we going to do? Every day there's less of me, and every day Mom needs more.

Plus, we're out of money.

Mom can't seem to hang onto a job.

I got a job after school. The cardboard box factory off Selleck Street needed a second-shift janitor. I actually enjoyed it. Being busy helps. Even emptying garbage and sweeping floors is good—too bad I can't empty my life so easily.

Came home at ten p.m. to find Mom hysterical.

"I told you I was going to work the afternoon shift, Mom, to earn some money." But she couldn't remember that we talked about it. She was absolutely insane with fear that I, too, had abandoned her. She waits for me after school. Stands at the door, staring down the road for my car. She expects me about twenty minutes after school's out, and today it was seven hours later than that.

It took me two hours to calm her down enough so we could both go to bed. I never did my homework. Had to wing it on both tests the next day.

I stared at Jennie during the tests. What is it like to have two parents who

A) think you're perfect,

B) are perfect themselves, and

C) have enough money to maintain all this perfection in style?

Jennie wrote the answers to the test questions as if she were writing a letter to her grandmother: her pencil just flowed along, like her brain, never slowing down, never forgetting.

I'm not as smart as Jennie. (But then, who is?) But it's not her brains I envy; it's her family.

I think of that Yuppie Yard sometimes—Jared and

Emily and Hillary and Jennie—with all their wall-to-wall perfection, and I'm jealous. I'm angry at Jennie because her parents love each other, and love her. Jennie flirts with me, and I walk away, because her life is perfect and my life is not.

Hillary Lang, her journal

I say to Emily, "Okay, Christmas. Spirit of love and all that. Joy. Hope. The whole thing. Got to be nice to Jennie, Star of the East."

Emily says, "Luckily I'm Jewish and don't celebrate Christmas."

We laugh insanely.

I say, "Spirit of Hanukah?"

Emily says, "Oh, yeah. Okay, let me write down what you said. Spirit of love, joy, and hope."

I say, "Why write it down? You afraid you'll forget the answer when the test comes?"

Emily says, "Listen. Just being with Jennie is a test these days."

And oh, it's true. We're talking a girl who no sooner finishes three performances of her own original musical than she gets A plus in all exams and demonstrates an original laser project in physics.

Emily says, "Stay calm, Hillary, two more days 'til Christmas break."

"Let's call it a Jennie break," I tell her.

We laugh: and The Awesome Twosome links arms and walks down the hall.

Every time a teacher announces that she is truly impressed with me, I lose a friend.

In physics we had to turn in our projects. I've been doing that experiment with the laser, and the teacher had me demonstrate it to the class. And Emily said, "A laser? You can't be a normal person and look up something boring in a library book? You have to come up with some dynamite experiment involving a laser?"

But the teacher says, "Emily, Jennie always reaches for the stars. It's a joy for a teacher to have a student like Jennie. Nobody else would have come up with this experiment." Emily's mouth forms a little *o* of rage and the teacher, who clearly thinks she has made us all feel better, turns to me, smiles gladly, and says, "Jennie, I'm truly impressed."

Emily rolled her eyes, yawned, looked out the window, and never glanced my way again.

I remember once when The Awesome Threesome all took clarinet lessons. I don't know why we picked the clarinet. Anyway, I was good, and Em and Hill were crummy. Hillary quit early on but Em played for years. She was never good, and she never much cared. "I like band," she would say, shrugging when she sat in the back with the beginners year after year.

"How can you stand it?" I said once. "Being ordinary at it?"

Emily was amazed. "Who cares?" she said.

Oh, why can't I feel that way? Why can't I just do something because I like it? Why do I have to be a winner at everything? How I envy the kids who don't even remember to study! What would it be like to live inside a body that's careless about things?

So after school today I went home alone because Em and Hill wouldn't wait for me.

I don't have much experience at being alone: not after a lifetime of The Awesome Threesome.

Piano practice, horseback riding, copying over my English paper—okay, you can do those alone. But Christmas shopping, alone? And try a phone call alone. There's another fun activity.

In the evening I had my harmony lesson. Music is like math, but it has more shape on the page. I love harmony. Tomorrow another test, an interview with the paper about being a young composer, jazz dancing class, and an evening rehearsal for *The Messiah* production.

We're going to visit Aunt Catherine on Saturday and on Sunday we're having a party for another set of people. Mother's theme isn't even Christmas: she's using pink. Pink? In December? I can't stand it when Mother gets trendy. I like tradition, nothing but tradition.

Mrs. Lang came over to lend Mother her large coffee-pot. I don't think she knows that Hillary doesn't speak to me anymore. I miss Hill so much I was all but clinging to Mrs. Lang.

My mother began to get nervous about all the things I still had to get done that day. "You mustn't hang about, Dunstan!" she cried. "Here's your list! Let's get cracking."

Mrs. Lang laughed. "There is only *one* thing you

have to do," she told me, tossing my full-page list aside. "You have to take the garbage out."

It was my turn to laugh. Only *one* thing I had to do? There were four hundred things I had to do. And I had to do them all well, too.

"Darling," said Mrs. Lang. "Spare time is the best time of all."

I've never even *seen* spare time. There is nothing my mother and father despise more. Starting with nursery school, they packed my life full, and since junior high, I've done my own packing.

Paul's diary

In gym we had athletic event tests: 400-yard dash, long jump, that kind of thing. Coach asked me again to go out for sports. God, how I'd like to! I feel so much better when I'm racing, or pulling, or even doing push-ups, or something. I'm all muscle, no thought: I don't worry, I don't remember, I don't even care: I just exist.

I didn't even answer him.

Someday it's going to start spilling out of me. I have this terrible fear it's going to be someplace public, with dozens of kids listening, and I'll be partly insane, and it'll pour out of me, every sordid detail, and I'll be this piece of public property, they'll all know every ounce of me.

I used to just stay quiet.

Now I try not to look at anybody, either. Meet their eyes and I feel myself starting to go.

Ansley's diary

Rumors spread so fast in this school. And somehow in the cafeteria Paul Classified got cornered. Really, it reminded me of animals: it was so primitive! It was exciting, like a hunt—and horrid, horrid. We should all have been shot ourselves.

Jared's been gossiping with some boys in gym (although Jared claims only girls "gossip"—boys "talk") and these guys have decided that Paul's family are spies: CIA, or something, and they cornered Paul and demanded to know what his parents do for a living. I mean, here's Paul having cream of tomato and a toasted cheese sandwich with four chocolate milks (all the boys drink these unbelievable amounts of milk) and there are six guys hunkering down around him, saying, "So, Paul R. Smith. So what exactly *are* all these secrets, anyway?"

And everybody is fascinated, and they start to get closer, so they can hear, and the cafeteria turns into a mob, half chanting, "So, Paul R. Smith. So who are you, Paul R. Smith?"

Paul stands up.

There isn't room for him to stand, so he shoves the whole table forward, catching three of the boys below the belt with the table rim. They yell, and Paul shoves the table harder, turning it over and spilling a bunch of lunches. Instantly we're all taking sides, shrieking for the side we like to fight, to win.

Even me.

Today I was part of a mob. I loved the wildness of it: the push and shove of it.

This is why the ancient Romans liked gladiators.

Fighting.

Animals. The animals you watch . . . *and the animals you become.*

When it was all over, and both the principals were in there, dragging Paul off his attackers, the people who were hardest to control were us—the ones staring and gaping and pushing up closer.

My skin was crawling.

Me. Ansley Augusta. Paul was attacked and I was a cheerleader to keep the violence going. I'm no different from any other creep.

Perhaps it's worth keeping a diary just to find that out.

Now I have to find Paul R.

And apologize.

JARED'S DIARY

Home: Dad is finally back from L.A. and the addition is started. They've decided to go to Colorado for a week over Christmas, but we'll be home in time for the New Year's party Ansley and I want to give. Mother isn't too thrilled about forty guests, but Ansley's parents agreed to help chaperone. Now I'm the one who isn't too thrilled. Oh, well.

Car: Got a speeding ticket. Makes it very hard to argue about chaperones at parties. I couldn't help driving fast. That Porsche engine roars under my foot and I go all crazy. Dad said maybe an old rusted four-cylinder beat-up olive green Plymouth is what I should be driving. Great, I said, I can trade cars with Paul Classified.

Weather: Winter. First snow didn't last. Second snow turned to rain.

School: Emily got a haircut. Very short. I like it. You see more of her face. Paul Classified got a three-day suspension for fighting. I swear to God Paul jerked up the table at exactly the angle to spill everybody's soup on my shirt. The whole thing was my fault, and I knew it and Ansley knew it and Paul Classified knew it. Ansley made me telephone him to apologize but thank God the guy has an unlisted phone number and I was saved from that little duty. The things a girl asks of you. Now she wants to celebrate a "Janiversary."

Paul Classified: Who would believe that some guy I don't even like would rate an entire diary category? But then who would believe that I am still trying to follow him? Billy Torello found out two facts. One, he has a little sister named Candy. Two, the little sister used to go to Talcott Hill Elementary School but she stopped going. Torello made this sound like a state secret.

"She probably just transferred to Country Day School," I said. Ansley would kill me if even more gossip got going and the guys had another fight with Paul.

"Party pooper," Hillary accused me. "I bet his sister Candy was kidnapped. Paul's parents are CIA agents, and they're being blackmailed by the KGB, who are holding Candy hostage until Mr. and Mrs. Smith obey their orders."

Great. That's the kind of rumor that started the cafeteria fight.

"Taken by the other parent in some vicious custody fight," guessed Keith, who has been there.

"Eaten by alligators," I said wearily. Anything to change the subject.

Misc.: Saw Jennie's pageant closing night. Her parents threw a magnificent party afterward. Everybody was there. Everybody except Paul. Of course Paul never goes anywhere except into hiding. I didn't see much of Hillary and Emily—they checked in and left. They must have a term paper due or something. But Mrs. Weinstein made the punch, and Hill's parents were there, and all seven kings and their families, and Miss Clinton, etc., etc., etc. Em's little brother Trip got a Polaroid camera for his birthday last week—he specialized in catching people chewing. Got a great shot of me choking on a celery stick—cream cheese all over my cheek. Ansley's going to frame it. I love you, too, I said to her.

Emily's diary

I had my hair cut. It's very short, and where it used to be limp now it's soft and wispy. I like it. It made me feel all excited to look in the mirror and see it: fluff instead of draperies. People are saying nice things. Maybe they're just being polite. But even Paul Classified commented on it, and I know Paul C. well enough by now to know he wouldn't rouse himself from silence just to lie about somebody's hair. So it must look good.

Hillary and I went to Jennie's gala event because it

would have been very hard to explain to our parents why we weren't there. A hundred people all hugging and congratulating Jennie. I took it for about ten minutes and left. It's a rerun: Jennie's a hit, Hill and I get jealous, Jennie goes on being a hit, so Hill and I walk out on her.

My little brother Trip's birthday party was the other day. He had his four best friends over and Mom took them skating and then they came home for cake. This four-layer cake she made herself, which she hasn't done in years, not since she went back to work, and immediately there is the problem of how do you cut a cake for five kids?

I think that's what Jennie is.

A birthday cake cut by an unfair mother.

I, Emily, got a sliver of cake and none of the really good icing. Hillary got a reasonable-sized piece, but nothing to write home about. Jennie got all the rest of the cake: the good flowers on top, the icing ribbons on the sides, and the thickest filling.

Oh, it's so unfair!

And the worst of it is, I'm a worse person. I'm not as nice as I was last year!

Jennie's diary

Closing night.
Awesome.
Applause.

Flowers from the cast.

A huge party at our house afterward: cast, orchestra, stagehands, teachers, and all their families and dates. Food, rock music, dancing, Christmas carols, and more food.

Mother bought me a splendid skirt: slippery shiny Christmas plaid to the floor, with a sexy, clingy black top and a wild crazy necklace, like a tree of silver and gold, and my earrings falling down to meet it—stars for me and my tree.

But what good is a perfect dress if Paul Classified doesn't see me in it?

What good is the best pageant and the greatest party if Emily and Hillary don't come?

You would think that joy could be shared more easily than anything else. After all, joy is the loveliest emotion. But joy is very difficult to hand around. You can't fling joy into the air like confetti and expect your friends to toss it with you when they don't have any of their own.

How did Mary the Mother of Jesus manage not to cry?

Or maybe she did cry. The Bible leaves out all the interesting parts. Did Mary cry forever? Did all the brothers and sisters and nieces and nephews of Jesus cry forever? Or did they bury him and get on with it, making supper and being carpenters?

I'm not even religious. I think the whole thing is a bunch of hooey. I have Christmas pageants on the brain.

Emily's diary

I need more money! I'm going to work a few evenings a week at McDonald's again.

An article about Jennie was in the paper Sunday. A full page of photographs of the pageant. Jennie taking a bow. Quotes from Miss Clinton saying Jennie is the most exciting student to go through Westerly High. The reporter obviously felt Jennie was the most wonderful possible example of young people today. A girl of absolute perfection, he wrote, what we all want our children to strive to be like.

Ugh.

Paul Classified won't have anything to do with her.

Everybody is getting sort of a kick out of it.

Here's Jennie, absolutely in love with him, her eyes all wide and starry whenever she sees him—and Paul Classified just stands there looking the other way and looking bored. Paul Classified is thinner. He used to have the perfect body. He doesn't now.

Catching Paul alone is impossible, he doesn't *do* alone.

But there are only a few days of school left before vacation and I'm really worried about him.

So I passed him a note in English class. *Dear Paul, I heard about the fight and I'm terribly sorry it happened. Listen, I'm not interfering or anything, but do you have anywhere to go on Christmas? I don't celebrate Christmas myself, but my mother and my little brother and I always go out for Christmas dinner anyhow, to keep from getting lonely on everybody else's holiday, and we would be happy to have you come with us. Love, Emily.*

He picked up his pen to write an answer but he didn't.

All through English class he stared down at my note. Jennie was very aware of the note and who it was from. Paul's face was different from usual: not closed off (Hillary says he has military security measures for his own face) but sad and open.

When class ended he drifted in the halls and let me drift up to him. I said, "We'd love to have you, Paul."

He said, "Thanks, Emily. It was nice of you to think about me. But my family needs me at home." He touched me—my cheek—and I looked up at him, but he was already going down the hall full speed. I never really thought about it until now, but I don't think Paul ever touched anybody before.

Just now, writing my diary, I realized something about that sentence. He didn't say his family would celebrate Christmas. Just that they needed him.

Paul's diary

I can't believe that of all the people in the world, I talked to Ansley Morgan. I don't even like Ansley. I don't like her world or her attitudes or her figure. But she apologized to me. She walked right up and said she was sorry about the fight, and that it was her fault and Jared's, and she would go with me to the principal if I wanted and get it straightened out. She said they had been playing games with my secrets and it was wrong.

"Yes," I said, "it was wrong."

"My journal for English has turned into a confessional," said Ansley. "You know what I mostly write down? The things I shouldn't have done." She slid her yellow hair out of her eyes and gave me a funny look. "I've got a really fat entry for you, Paul."

I shrugged. But I didn't walk away from her. It's funny. Ansley is honest. What you see is what you get. There aren't that many people in the world you can say that about. All of a sudden I envied Jared.

Ansley changed the subject to school sports, and then to weather, and I said suddenly, "You're the only one who has never quizzed me, Ansley."

"Because I will never let anybody quiz me, either," she said, her eyes sparkling so that for one moment she looked like Jennie. "I'm going to keep my smile and my preppy clothes and my money between me and curiosity. You've got a right to your privacy, Paul."

I almost fell off my chair at that one. Maybe she didn't know Jared was following me.

Then she leaned way forward, really sparkling now, and said in a very teasing voice, "Although there is one thing I'm truly dying to know, Paul."

"What's that?"

"What does the 'R.' stand for?"

He actually told me. But it was sweet, not horrid. "Revere." He was named by his real mother—that's the phrase he used—his "real" mother—for Paul Revere. For the midnight ride of Paul Revere. "She was a real mother," he said. "She wanted her son to have a midnight ride of his own. Cure cancer or bring peace in the Middle East or discover a nuclear deterrent."

His mother is dead, I thought, absolutely shaken. It's grief and despair keeping him so solitary and so hidden. And to think we've teased him about all this when he just buried his own mother! I said quickly, "I'm sure you'll do one of those things, Paul."

He laughed, choking on his own laugh, and looked away from me, and then I realized it's not his mother who's the problem—it's him! He's got leukemia or something and he won't do something immortal because he won't have time! I grabbed his arm and I said, "Paul, you're not sick, are you? You aren't dying or something, are you? You're all right, aren't you?"

He gave me a sweet smile, and said, "No, thanks, Ansley. I'm fine."

Of course now I really *do* want Jared to follow him everywhere and find out what's going on. Has somebody died? Is somebody dying? What is the midnight ride of this particular Paul Revere supposed to be, anyhow?

O, Ansley Augusta Morgan.
You are bad, bad, bad.
And curious, curious, curious.
And determined, determined, determined.

Jennie's diary

All day I have thought about stars: real stars—sky stars.

I am so lonely I am the reverse of a star: I am a black hole in space.

In English today I leaned over to Hillary and Emily and whispered, "I just can't wait for vacation, can you? I can't wait to go skiing. I heard on the radio they just got seven more inches of snow at Killington."

Hill was wearing a new sweatshirt with weird little reindeer running after a disappearing Santa Claus. It was not in Christmas colors, but in yellow and lime green and turquoise. You kept staring at it, wondering whether you loved it or hated it. I remember when the Awesome Three-some did all their shopping together: we were never the same sizes, but we could always exchange tops. Last year I would have said, "Hill! It's crazy! When do I get to wear it?" This year I didn't even know what stores she liked. I certainly hadn't gone with her. Killington, I thought, some-how, some way, we'll put it back together on the ski slopes.

Hillary examined her fingernails. Mine are bitten to the quick—hers are lovely, long, and polished. Hillary looked at Emily and Emily looked at her desk, and Hillary said, "I think our vacation plans are somewhat different this year, Jennie. Just Emily and I are going."

She said it out loud.

The whole room heard.

And all the people who usually watch Paul Classified, picking up clues, watched me. I don't know what they saw. I wasn't even inside my body again for hours: I was just this thing sitting upright, hanging onto the sobs, waiting for the day to end.

But my days never end.

And I even had to ride home with them. I thought I would crumble, like a stale cookie. We didn't exchange a single sentence.

I got out, they drove on, Emily got out, and from the doorway Em's mother said, "Darling. Come give me a hug."

I went inside and my mother met me at the door, crying, "Dunstan! Dunstan! Tell me what you did today, dear!"

What if I didn't do anything today?

What if I just existed, like Hillary and Emily?

What would my mother do?

Would she still love me?

I hid my tears. "You can yell Dunstan until your throat is raw, Mother, and I'm going to wait until you say Jennie."

"But Jennie is so common," she said fretfully. "How was I to know every third girl in the school system would be named Jennie?"

"Mother, Dunstan sounds like a dead king in Shakespeare."

"It's your middle name. It has character."

"It'll have to have character without me," I said. I

pushed past her into the house, almost flinging my books at the wall. I could just see myself telling Hillary and Emily they have to call me Dunstan.

"But Dunstan Quint sounds so exciting!" cried my mother. "It'll look so successful when the pageant is published." She dragged me into the dining room. The entire room is me: from my kindergarten crayon pictures framed in red to my junior-high piano recital programs framed in a tailored black. She and Daddy had framed the first page of my pageant manuscript. The frame was so massive, so ornate, so gold—you'd think it was Beethoven up there over the fireplace, not my little Christmas piece.

"It's nice," I managed.

She told me I was tired and I would feel better after dinner.

I doubted that a hot meal would bring back a friendship.

The dining-room table is always beautifully set. Mother likes a formal meal. Our house was photographed once in *House Beautiful.* I was ten, and Mother dressed me in a long colonial gown with a starched white apron and a tiny white cap and perched me in the antique chairs like a prop that breathed.

I gave Daddy a kiss, and sat down. We said grace together, as we always do, and as she always does, Mother smiled and said proudly, "Such a nice family."

As if we were a trophy.

A display case of nice family.

"Jennie, darling, are you upset about something?" My mother was mystified. What on earth would her Jennie have to be upset about?

I took the plunge. "My friendship with Hillary and Emily is sort of petering out," I said, which was the understatement of the year.

"We all saw it coming, Jennie," my father said. He took some chicken and passed the gravy. "Hillary and Emily are fine girls, but average. You're just not going to be associating with that kind of girl as you grow up. I know you feel sad about The Awesome Threesome, but the truth is, Hill and Em would just hold you back."

Life is good.

No friends to hold me back.

What a treat.

"Emily must be such a disappointment to Margaret," said my mother. "I mean, Em is a happy child, and of course that's greatly to be admired, but one always hopes one's child will be an achiever. Em simply exists."

"Mrs. Weinstein is very proud of Emily," I said stiffly.

"I don't know why. Name one thing Em has accomplished since she started high school."

Accomplished, I thought.

"See? You can't think of a thing." Mother smiled into her crystal goblet as if it foretold our lives. "Emily probably will end up going to the University of Connecticut. Hillary may not even get in there."

"Mother, UConn is a perfectly good school."

"Certainly. For ordinary people."

I pictured Paul Classified throwing the table at those boys. I had a terrible fierce desire to throw the table at my mother. In my lap I clung to my napkin. I forced myself to finish chewing and swallow and have a sip of water. "I was talking to Miss Clinton today about my next musical," I said. I didn't want to talk music. I wanted to talk Hillary and Emily, friends and losses. But my parents were *glad* that I'm losing Hill and Em. They didn't *care* if I didn't have a single friend!

Daddy is lean and gray and tired from the commute to New York. The family rule is to talk about pleasant things. What I do every day is always a pleasant thing to Daddy. I don't know much about what he does. He dislikes talking about his own work. "Have you written much of the dialogue yet?" he asked.

"I have the title in mind. But I don't have much experience with dialogue, Daddy."

"Not a whole lot of dialogue you can throw into a Christmas pageant," agreed Daddy. "After you've said 'no room at the inn' you've about finished up the speeches."

I had Thanksgiving in mind.

I'd been reading diaries of Puritans and Pilgrims. The sentence that stuck in my head was, "Ye season, it was winter."

How cold it felt. How on the edge of that terrible wilderness! How hungry and bleak and dark. *Ye Season It Was Winter*. I could feel them all, in their shabby wraps, huddled around inadequate fires in drafty huts, trying to believe they would survive. *Ye Season It Was Winter*.

Over the summer, writing the pageant, I was full of enthusiasm. While Hillary was in Switzerland and Emily was making Happy Meals, I was filled with excitement, as if I were a thermos, and all the cups were music.

Now the thermos is empty. Emily and Hillary are just mad at me for not telling them what I was doing on the pageant. But if I *had* told them, they would have been even madder! Hill would have said, "You can't sew seven kings' costumes!" and Emily would have said, "A whole musical? Get out of town. You can't do all that."

But I *can* do it!

And if I can do it once, I can do it twice!

But I can't get excited over anything without friends.

I guess that's why I'm clinging to my crush on Paul Classified. I can pretend to this diary that at least *he's* my friend.

55

"Not my favorite meal, dear," Daddy said to Mother. "I know Jennie likes chicken and biscuits, but why don't you make that wonderful shrimp-stuffed eggplant you served the Farrells last month?"

"Oh, yes! *The New York Times Cookbook*. Yes, and perhaps we'll ask the Benjamins to dinner. I think they could be of considerable assistance in Jennie's career."

I hate eggplant. I hate shrimp. I don't much like the Benjamins, either. And I don't want a career. I want friends.

Daddy was beaming. "While girls like Hillary and Emily are busy trying on clothes at Bloomingdale's, you, my dear, are becoming a serious composer."

Serious composer. It sounds so sober. Full of frowns and silence.

"I can hardly believe your junior year is half over, Jennie," said my father. "Time to start thinking of colleges. With your record you can go anywhere. Harvard if you want academics. Juilliard if you want music only."

We sat at the table—another trio—as if they thought the trio of Quints could replace the trio of Emily, Hill, and Jennie. Above us, framed in gold, hung the first page of my pageant orchestration: black notes rushing across the staff, a row of treble clefs where I practiced the shape of them, and margin notes where Miss Clinton helped me.

Neither my mother nor my father looked at me.

Their eyes were glued to the manuscript.

"I feel as if we've gone on safari," my father said, laughing, turning at last to smile at me.

"Safari?" I repeated. My father is the least likely person in Connecticut to go on a safari. He is strictly New York City.

"As if we went to Africa and bagged a great specimen," he said, beaming. "We bagged a daughter who comes in first."

56

Paul's diary

I dedicate myself to having no profile at all and I end up with a profile so high that people *follow* me when I drive off!

—— —— —— —— Jared followed me again.

I'll draw lines instead of writing the four-letter words. Saying those words is like any other kind of talking: I'm afraid once I begin, I'll never stop. How would it be to swear for all eternity?

We got to a red light, and I leaped out of my car and ran back past three other cars and ripped open the driver's door of his shiny red Porsche. I hung onto the handle so I wouldn't rip open the shiny blue ski jacket he was wearing. "Where do you get off?" I screamed at him. "I do not exist in order to put excitement into your little yuppie life!" But I didn't stay for an answer. The light turned green, I raced back to my car, drove off about a hundred miles an hour, and never saw the Porsche again.

I had to quit the factory job. Mom can't make it without me home after school. I'd like to know how we're both going to make it unless one of us is earning money.

Emily's diary

Jealousy hurts me, because I'm the one who is bad enough to feel it, but today I saw my own jealousy cutting Jennie.

She actually begged us to be her friends.

We had reached Hillary's car and were on the way home via Bloomingdale's, because Hill had some last-minute shopping. She forgot her cousins. We were thinking about scarves, because you can always use a scarf, but scarves are boring—who wants to open a package and find yet another scarf?

And Jennie came running across the parking lot and jumped into the back seat.

We just sat in the front without talking to her.

"May I have a ride home?" she asked.

Hill looked at her in the rearview mirror. "We aren't going straight home, Jennie."

Jennie was nervous. She could compose a whole musical, but she couldn't be our friend, and she knew it. "Oh. Where are you going?"

I knew we were going to be mean. I could feel it, and I didn't even stop. I wanted to be mean, just the way she wants to show off and be better than anybody else. Hillary said, "What business is it of yours, Jennie? The Awesome Threesome doesn't exist anymore, you know, and you can't just go jumping into other people's cars as if you owned them."

Even I gasped at that. But I didn't say anything nice, either.

Jennie screamed, "What do you want of me? Do you want me to be stupid? Okay, I'll fail a class. Do you want me to be ugly? Okay, I'll stop washing my hair. Do you want me to be boring? Okay, I'll never say an interesting sentence again! Will you like me then?"

I was stone.

Hill was ice.

Jennie was raw, bleeding flesh.

But stone and ice don't respond, and Hill and I didn't respond to Jennie, and Jennie, sobbing, leaped out of the car and slammed the door and ran back to the high school.

Half of me thought, *Good, we hurt her.*

And the other half of me thought, *Oh my God, we hurt her!*

Paul's diary

Now the guys are really fascinated. Anybody who'll fight back a half dozen of them, and then win a round with Dr. Sykes—it must be some secret he's protecting.

I want to pound their faces in.

The CIA. Spies.

Give me a break. Do they think I like living like this? Do they think I want secrets in my life? I hate this! I want my life normal and boring and routine like other people's.

And if I tell them the "secret" (secret? It's my *life*, not a secret!) they'd be disappointed. They want it to be romantic.

Romantic's a funny word. It means adventure, and thrills, and heart-stopping journeys: fast cars and small planes and wild beasts: spies and cold wars, dead bodies and codes.

My life?

Hah.

My life is a sister I could kill.

My life is a mother who has collapsed. I get to be the one who will put her in an institution. That should be romantic, huh?

Okay, okay. Take a deep breath. One more day until vacation.

It won't be a vacation for me. Just no school. Home all day long? How am I going to make it?

Jennie's diary

Lonely has a temperature.

Cold.

Paul Classified doesn't even look at me now.

It hurts so much!

I feel as if it's a lesson from God. I thought I could have everything, so God picked out something I can't have, and every minute of every day, He puts Paul in front of me so I have to gaze at what I can't have.

The Awesome Threesome is gone. Now there is a twosome. Emily and Hillary. I think it's still awesome. Friendship itself is awesome. Wonderful—miraculous—to be wanted for your company.

Nobody wants mine, and I'm shedding some pretty awesome tears about it, too. But I have no awesome solutions. I have no solutions at all.

Emily's diary

Don't tell, Paul begged me.

We're standing there at the emergency room door and he takes my hand—like he's my subject, I'm his lord—and pleads with me. "Don't tell, Emily." I try to reason with him. I try to explain that people can help, that he'll do better, feel better, end up better, if people know.

But he's standing there: his 170 pounds, his six feet, his broad shoulders, his thick dark hair, his fingers twice as wide as mine—and he's fragile. He could break.

So I promise.

"I won't tell," I whisper back.

He leans against the wall, kind of puffing out his breath in little gasps, as if he'd just run a great distance.

I said, "But what will you do? You can't live alone."

"Easier than living together," said Paul shortly.

He looked at me with terrible tension—all the wires in him stretched taut—and I promised again not to tell.

I'm not even writing it down. I just realized that a diary is very exposed. You may think there is privacy in one, but there isn't, and now it's not my life I'm talking about—it's Paul's.

Jennie's diary

If I am admired as one who achieves, Ansley and Jared are admired simply because they exist. To go to their parties is to have a front-row seat in the auditorium of life.

"You're coming to my New Year's party, of course," said Jared. He put his arm around me. I like affection as much as the next girl, but Jared's embrace never means affection; it's just part of his stance, as if we're about to be photographed.

But oh, how glad I was to be invited. I, Jennie Quint, top of the mountain, top of the pile, cream of the crop—I almost wept because someone wanted my company.

"Bring a date," said Jared. "Who are you going out with right now, Jennie?"

Nobody. But I want to be with Paul Classified. Paul's arms around me, Paul's kiss on my lips. I would have to catch him in class. If only there were a time and a place when I could talk privately to Paul. But P.C. is crafty: he can protect his secrets best in a crowd.

Ansley sauntered down the hall toward us. Ansley has a wonderful walk: she never hurries and yet she always gets places faster than anybody else. I've tried a hundred times to imitate that walk and can't. Ansley tossed her hair: thick pale yellow hair. Ansley had it cut so that it would fall over her left eye, and Ansley could fling it back. Slowly, it would slither down over the eye again. Very effective. Sexy.

"Coming to our party, darling?" said Ansley.

You have to live in a certain place and your parents have to have a certain income to be Ansley's darling. Jared never calls anybody "darling." Except maybe himself. "You inviting Hill and Emily?" I asked.

"No, I don't think so. Hill and Em just aren't very exciting, you know what I mean?"

I came to their defense as if there were still an Awesome Threesome. "So what's your idea of excitement? All you ever do is buy clothes, Ansley. Is excitement the January sales?"

But Ansley just laughed.

Fifth period, incredibly, I managed to be alone with Paul Classified. He actually agreed to abandon language lab for the library. Sitting in one of the carrels, we were supposedly working on German together. German poets of the nineteenth century. In German. I can only assume I signed up for this course when I was insane. Paul, in fact, *was* working on his German. I was working on Paul. "Ansley and Jared are giving a party," I said casually.

Paul Classified's face moved slightly: not really a smile, but maybe it was meant to be. "I forget sometimes you live in the Yuppie Yard with all that crowd. You're so different from them, Jennie." He shook his head, as though the difference were so vast you would have to shade your eyes in the sun to see across the gap.

"I never heard anybody call it the Yuppie Yard before."

Paul was amazed. "That's the nickname for all those ritzy little lanes off Talcott Hill," he said.

"Where do you live, anyhow?"

"Downtown." He flipped through the index in the German book without looking anything up. "The pageant went well, Jennie. I was impressed."

I forgave him for not telling where he lived. "What night did you come?"

The pageant ran three nights. Standing ovations all three nights. Talk of Young Composer of the Year Award. Talk of scholarships to a conservatory like Juilliard, or having the music published.

But no talk with Emily or Hillary.

There was a momentary pause. Hardly unusual for Paul. But the answer—*oh, the answer!* That was unusual. "All three nights," he said. He was not looking at me. He was staring into the German book index. Paul drew in a deep breath, and his fingers tightened on his pencil. Paul who never fidgeted bit his lips and wet them with his tongue and did not look my way.

All three nights? Paul Classified, who did not play sports, did not go to assemblies, did not attend concerts, did not go to parties—Paul went all three nights to my Christmas pageant? Plus the dress rehearsal?

My heart was pounding harder than language lab could ever make it do. I wanted to take a break from flirting with him and race through the halls and find Emily and Hill and tell them all the details.

And then I remembered. The last thing Emily and Hillary wanted to know was that I had triumphed yet again.

Paul and I went back to the German. We translated another paragraph. When we flipped to the back of the book to check an unknown word, my hand brushed against Paul Classified's.

I took a deep breath. I had not known how scary it would be actually to ask the question. "Would you like to go with me to Jared and Ansley's party, Paul?"

His eyes stayed on the index. His hand lay flat on the pages. His face went back to its shuttered look: the one where I no longer know if he's handsome or plain, interesting or dull. "I'm sorry, Jennie," he said. "My family has plans. I can't make it. But thank you for asking me."

How do you know they have plans? I didn't tell you what day the party is.

Paul Classified went on translating, as if it mattered.

How could he have turned me down?

How could he have wanted to hear my pageant three times but not want to go out with me?

The pounding in my heart got worse because I wanted to run away. But I had to sit there, being exactly like Paul R. Smith. Being nothing important to anyone.

I can't tell Em and Hill about the good things in my life. I have too many. They're jealous. But I can share the bad things. They'd like that. I can tell them Paul Classified turned me down, and that will make them happy.

But what a price to pay!

Is that what life requires?

You can have two friends again, kid, as long as you agree not to get Paul.

Paul's diary

McDonald's.

Now if that isn't a normal everyday unthreatening place, what is? You wouldn't think your life could collapse at a McDonald's. I even chose the one in Stamford so we wouldn't run into anyone we knew.

Wrong. Emily has a job there. Emily got our order.

Of course Mom could not have looked worse. She went to her new job today, but she didn't dress right, and there are terrible circles under her eyes, and I couldn't talk her into putting on makeup or brushing her hair. I wanted to tell Emily—Mom didn't used to look like this! She used to be pretty and she used to laugh.

Emily was all bright and cheerful, of course: partly McDonald's behavior to customers, and partly Emily. She beamed at us. Her hair was pretty: soft, cloudy. I thought that after I paid for the hamburgers I would tell her that. Emily said, "Hi, Paul. Is this your Mom? Hi, Mrs. Smith."

My mother started crying.

Right there at the McDonald's.

Patrons six deep at five lines, and my mother is sobbing on the counter.

Emily looked at my mother in horror, and then at me.

I closed my eyes for a minute to get strength. I didn't get any. "Mom, pull yourself together," I whispered. Please God, please let her stop crying. I can't even take this at home, how can I take it in front of fifty people at McDonald's?

My mother just shook her head and kept on sobbing. She didn't make a whole lot of noise, but she went limp, as if she planned to take a nap on top of the brown tray where Emily had put a Christmas placemat.

We had to get out of there. "Mom, let's go back to the car," I said, trying not to scream, because if Mom panicked it would just get worse.

People were staring at us. "Is she having a fit or something?" demanded a fat woman next to us, pulling away in case it was catching. The line we were in dissolved. Customers moved to other registers. People who were afraid of fits looked away, and people who weren't stared as hard as they could.

The manager came scurrying out. "Can I help you,

ma'am?" My mother just lay there. By now nobody was talking, not the customers, not the McDonald's crew, and most of all not me. The manager was about eighteen years old and terrified of women collapsing on his counters.

By now I knew that if I was going to move my mother, I'd have to pick her up. I'm trying to stay in control, right? I'm trying not to yell at her or at the strangers around us, I'm trying to get her out of there. She's not doing anything but sobbing. All of a sudden I know I'm going to fall apart, too. I can't think or move.

Emily said to the manager, "Steve, take my register." She came around, put an arm under my mother, and said to me, "Let's get her into the ladies' room, Paul." All I could think of was that Emily would have to go into the ladies' room with her—for a whole minute, maybe two, I would not have to be responsible. We got out of line and staggered to a table back by the restrooms, folding my mother into one of those plastic chairs. I held Mom up by the shoulders while Emily knelt on the other side and rubbed Mom's hands. All I wanted to do was go home forever.

"Do you want me to call an ambulance?" asked Emily quietly.

An ambulance? It wasn't like Mom was bleeding or anything.

Emily kept supporting my mother, but she put her hand on mine. It was warm, and large, and her fingers were fingers that work hard: not elegant, not pretty, but strong. "My father used to be drunk all the time," she said. Her voice was very calm, as if she had done this for years. After her next sentence I knew she had. "We used to have to go to the railroad station and scrape him up off the parking lot into the back seat."

"She's not drunk," I managed to say. "She's having a nervous breakdown."

"Oh, Paul," said Emily, and her eyes filled with tears. Tears for me. I picked up the saltshaker with my free hand and felt the hard edges of it. "Listen, Paul, with my father the only thing that worked was to get him into an institution. *You* can't be responsible. It'll kill you."

"I have to be responsible," I said. "There isn't anyone else." I tried to crush the saltshaker in my hand but I couldn't quite do it. If my father had been around I would have crushed him, but I couldn't do that, either.

Emily blew out her breath hard. "Well, I guess I have some of the answers, Paul Classified. I know why you're thinner. I know why you're always clamming up. But what they taught us in Al-Anon is, the first step is talking about it."

"I told you, she isn't drunk."

"Paul, I believe you. Anyway, I remember the smell too well. But she looks half dead. You do, too. And I'm serious about the ambulance. Maybe she needs to be in the psychiatric ward at the hospital."

My mother wasn't even listening. She could have been a very large rag doll.

"If you get her home like this, then what'll you do?" said Emily practically.

Her hand was still on mine. It was comforting. But I changed the subject. "What happened to your father, Emily?"

She shrugged. "Mom divorced him, he's remarried twice, he's very handsome, you know, very dashing when he's not on a binge. He really isn't part of our lives any more. It's terrible, it still hurts us all. But there you are, these things happen and you have to get past them."

I couldn't believe she talked about it. I can't *stand* talking about it.

"Is that all?" Emily said then. "Is that the secret, Paul? Your mother fell apart?"

I ended up telling her the whole thing. My real mother, my real sister, my real father. Three people abandoning us was too much. "Mom couldn't take it," I finished. "Something in her snapped."

Emily listened, keeping her hand where it was, like a lifeline. "When you say Mom, you mean your stepmother?"

I shrugged. "Only mother I had. Biological doesn't count."

But oh, it counted for Candy! She wrote off her whole childhood and walked out the door with a strange person who said, oh by the way, I'm your mother. And Mom, Mom died inside when Candy abandoned us.

I didn't say that to Emily. But maybe she knew. She told the kid manager to call the ambulance. She went with me to the hospital. She gave me lots of advice I didn't listen to. She promised not to talk, but what is a promise? Nobody I know ever kept one.

I went home to an empty house. I'd forgotten to get the hamburgers. I was starving. What a great guy you are, I thought. You just checked your mother into the psychiatric ward, and all you can think of is a Big Mac.

That was yesterday.

Today I avoided Emily like the plague.

I couldn't stand to look at her or think about her.

So I ended up closeted with Jennie Quint.

It was so crazy. Jennie's flirting, I'm trying to survive; Jennie's asking me to a New Year's party, I'm wondering if there will *be* a New Year.

Emily's diary

I am, after all, the girl who knows Paul's secrets.

But it's just your typical sad sordid suburban secret, and if he'd talked about it all along, it wouldn't hurt so much and he wouldn't be so alone.

But what do I do now? It's Christmas vacation, and we're off to Killington and Paul is alone. I tried to telephone him. It's been disconnected. I phoned the hospital to ask after Mrs. Smith, but they wouldn't give me any information at all. I have to help Paul, and I have to help Mrs. Smith—but I promised I wouldn't tell.

What is a promise?

How much does it count?

How bad are you if you keep the promise and how bad are you if you break it?

Ansley's diary

It's noisy out. Isn't that odd? Ice clinging to every twig has cracked, dropping through the crust of snow. Shutters tap, branches rasp together, and the wind whistles out of tune behind the shed.

Mrs. Quint was over talking to Jared's mother. It seems that her dear brilliant special Jennie had a hard holiday. Mrs. Quint is angry at Emily and Hillary for abandoning Jennie, even though Mrs. Quint has never liked Em and Hill. Mrs. Quint feels the world should revolve around her precious Jennie and she is absolutely frosted about this mediocre Christmas.

Jared and I had a perfect holiday. Everybody should spend a winter vacation in Colorado. Got home December 30, threw our bags down and went into New York for the day. We got tickets to *Amahl and the Night Visitors*. It's kind of sentimental but I like that musical: crippled boy receives miracle when he gives his only possession—his crutch—to the infant King.

I was thinking, though.

You feel sorry for Amahl because he's pitiful.

If Amahl were perfect—like Jennie—then you wouldn't care.

Perfect people are on their own.

Jennie's diary

Two weeks ago I told Dad about *Ye Season, It Was Winter*. Already he wants to see what I've gotten accomplished. Sometimes I feel as if I'm under attack.

But I keep producing, I keep working, I keep doing my best. I love doing my best. It makes me feel shiny inside, and breathless.

And I want to talk about it.

71

I want to call Hillary up and shriek, "Hill! I did it again! And it's good!" I want to call Emily up and yell, "Em! Wait 'til you read this! I'm brilliant!"

Can you imagine? They'd hang up on me. Then they'd call each other up. *"Do you believe that conceited arrogant blankety blank Jennie Quint?"*

But it hardly matters.

They went to Killington the day after Christmas.

Jared and Ansley went to Colorado to ski.

Nobody knows what Paul Classified did. I guess he likes being alone. He certainly has the choice of friends and parties. I can't imagine that. Why ever on earth would a person choose to be alone? I hate being alone!

Daddy and Mother got worried about me because I was depressed, so we flew out to Chicago to visit Daddy's college friends for a weekend. Chicago was fun. It looks the way a city should look. Daddy brought tapes of the musical and his old college roommate thinks we can get it published. Mother went wild with excitement and got right to work on the leads he provided.

I would love it—and yet—how could I tell anybody?

They don't want me to do more, they want me to do less.

January

Hillary Lang, her journal

The Awesome Threesome went cross-country skiing on the hills beyond Lost Pond. There had been an ice storm, and skiing was crunchy. We were together five hours.

Marching orders from our mothers, actually, because over Christmas vacation we're not allowed to be mean. I said to my mother, "Did Mrs. Quint tell you to tell us to ask Jennie?" and my mother said, "Are you kidding? Mrs. Quint is thrilled that Jennie is finally out of the threesome. It was holding Jennie back, you know."

And I said, "So why do Emily and I have to do this?" and my mother said, "Because I felt so guilty at Killington without Jennie that I had a horrible time."

I rolled my eyes. "*You* have a horrible time and *I* have to be nice?" I said. My mother shrugged. "Life isn't fair," she reminded me. I rolled my eyes again. "Of course not," I told her. "After all, we're talking Jennie here."

So we invited Jennie skiing and she was happy. Emily, however, was weird. I hated it. It isn't like Emily to be weird. Em is so ordinary, it's what I like best about her. Some of the time it was me and Jennie talking, with Emily just being weird in between topics. Something that interests all three of us is Paul Classified, but even then Emily was weird.

"What do you think Paul Classified's background really is, anyhow?" I said.

"Maybe one of his parents is in prison," said Jennie. "That's why he won't tell us anything about himself."

"He doesn't look like the sort of person with a parent in prison," I objected.

"I know, but have you ever seen his parents?"

"No," I admitted. "I don't think anybody has."

And does Emily contribute her ideas about Paul Classified? No. Emily says, "Look up Talcott Hill. Every sliver of ice is a prism tossing off sunlight."

"Paul's an alien," was my next suggestion. "He doesn't have parents. He's a collection of atomic particles."

Jennie giggled. "Actually I wouldn't be surprised if he's a spy. Has a second passport under a false name and Swiss bank accounts to turn to in time of trouble."

"The false name," I said, "is the one we have. Paul Smith? Now I ask you. Can anybody really be named Paul Smith?"

"Paul *R.* Smith," corrected Jennie. "Let's not forget the classified initial."

Emily actually said, out loud, and everything, "The sky is so blue it's not part of the world. Isolated as Paul. Come spring, maybe the sky will soften and get involved again."

Jennie and I stared at her, and then at the sky. Jennie said, "I like that, Em. The sky as uninvolved politics."

Well, maybe Jennie liked it, but I didn't. I went back to Paul Classified. Taking off my ski gear and leaning it up against the back porch, I said, "I think the 'R' stands for some horrible name, like Rollo or Reginald." The three of us went into my house thinking of humiliating "R" names. There were a lot. Roscoe. Rudolph. "Enough to make anybody decide his middle name is classified information," said Jennie, giggling.

My mother greeted us with hugs and kisses and hot chocolate. "How was skiing? Did you have a good time? Why didn't you ask me to go along? You're so mean, you three. You never include me." She was just babbling. She was so pleased that the three of us had lasted four hours without coming apart at the seams. Cross-country is hard work. It helps when you're gasping for breath, you can't argue much. And it was nice that we had an ice storm— Jennie fell as much in the ice as we did.

"Next time, Ma. This time I instructed you to stay in the kitchen making cookies and apple pie for us. Did you obey me?"

We all laughed. Mom is a computer analyst in the city and hasn't baked a cookie since I started first grade. "No," she said, "but I rented some good movies. I told the man I wanted a movie to cry by. I am in the mood for tears and Kleenex."

"On New Year's Day?" said Jennie. "That sounds very significant to me, Mrs. Lang."

"I'm going to get all my sobbing for the year over with the first day," she explained.

So we trooped into the family room and convinced my father that he really wanted to see his football game in the bedroom on the little TV. After sticking the tearjerker in the VCR, The Awesome Threesome lay on the rug to eat bakery cookies and drink instant hot chocolate while my mother tucked herself under an afghan and prepared to sob for an hour and a half.

But I was the one who sobbed.

Later. Much later.

When everybody was gone, and the movie was over, and my parents went out: then I sobbed for an hour and a half. I was terrible, so terrible, I was bad, every ounce of me, I actually *hated* another person.

On New Year's Day.

Emily's diary

Don't tell includes Hillary.

I can't talk to Hillary! Or my mother! Or Hill's parents. Who are practically my second set anyhow.

Don't tell. I didn't realize how much Classified was asking. He's asking me to become classified, too.

What a test. Doing everything with Hillary, including talking about Paul Classified—and not breathing a word. I don't think I've ever kept a secret before. I don't think I've ever *had* a secret before. Not from Hill.

Mrs. Lang made us be nice to Jennie and I think Hill and I were both secretly glad. It's easier to be nice when you're under orders. And I even had a pretty good time. But they kept bringing Paul up! And I kept having to bite my tongue to keep from telling what I know! Instead I would say something dumb about the sky or the glare off the snow.

I was so glad when we went inside for hot chocolate; Mrs. Lang would do all the talking now and I was off the hook.

But Mrs. Lang wanted us all to write New Year's resolutions. "I don't think a person should go overboard," she said, tossing pencils at us. "Three is probably enough. Let's write three New Year's resolutions apiece." We agreed, and Mrs. Lang handed everybody an index card. "So your resolutions won't be too long," she explained.

"What are you going to resolve, Mom?" said Hillary.

"Same thing I resolve every year. One, be more patient with my teenage daughter. Two, be superwoman and go back to baking cookies so my teenage daughter won't complain that we are single-handedly supporting all the bakeries in town. Three, read the Great Books I've been meaning to read since I was in college."

We gave her a round of applause. I adore Mrs. Lang.

I wondered what Mrs. Smith was like, before her nervous breakdown. I wondered if she could go back to being the old Mrs. Smith. I wondered if Paul had sat home alone for the whole vacation.

And all of a sudden I knew who could help.

"I, personally," said Hillary, "have an all-new, improved, and higher-quality list of resolutions. The new me is going to be a particularly spectacular new me," she explained.

"Yeah?" I said, running away from my own thoughts. I felt heavy with my secrets. "Lemme see your list." I grabbed Hill's index card and read it out loud. "Hillary Lang, her list. One, lose seven pounds."

We all giggled.

"Now that's precise, Hill. Not five, not ten, but seven pounds. You've measured your fat? You know that seven pounds from now you will be in a state of perfection?"

"Just keep reading," said Hillary with dignity. "And don't say it, Jennie, I can see your clever little brain noticing that I am on my fifth cookie. Refrain from commenting on that, okay?"

"Okay," said Jennie meekly. We were all on our best behavior. There was nothing awesome about the Threesome except that it had gotten back together for an afternoon of skiing.

I read Hill's second resolution out loud. "Two, get a B in physics." I thought: *Mr. Lowe! Jared's father! He could do anything!*

"Get a B in physics!" echoed Mrs. Lang. "Now there's a goal. I am impressed, Hillary, darling. You are such an unexpected person to live with. Who would have thought that the second most important thing in your life is a B in physics?"

"It isn't the second most important thing in my life," protested Hill. "It isn't even the twenty-second most important thing in my life. It's just a resolution that happened to come to me."

Mr. Lowe is one of those important lawyers who get quoted in the *Wall Street Journal* and are always flying off to Europe or Washington or Tokyo to consult on something or other. I don't care about that. But a person who can help the president solve world legal problems—he could do something about Paul.

I looked at Hillary's third resolution, and my heart stopped. I wanted to skip over it, but Mrs. Lang read it out loud over my shoulder. "Three, learn the truth about Paul Classified."

Hillary thinks Paul's secret is spies and high adventure: traitorous sales of computer chips to the Soviet Union, with pressure put on the family by kidnapping sweet innocent little Candy. Ansley thinks that Paul may have a dread disease, Billy Torello thinks that Paul's family sells drugs.

Paul was just left holding the bag. When we went through all that horror with my father, and all his drinking problems, I had my mother, and all four of my grandparents, and a bunch of cousins and friends to take me through it. Paul has nobody.

I give Paul credit. When everyone else abandoned Mrs. Smith, he wouldn't.

I don't have a crush on Paul Classified any more. I just plain love him. For his sense of responsibility. What an odd reason to love.

"Paul Classified will never tell us a thing," I said firmly. "Now listen up, everybody, because here are *my* resolutions." I used my TV commentator's voice, to make my list sound as important as Central American politics. "Emily Weinstein, her list. One, be nicer to my disgusting, revolting little brother. Two, get on honor roll and stay there. Three, go out with Donny Donnelly."

"Ooooh, you like *him?*" said Hillary in disgust.

I have no interest in Donny whatsoever, it was just a name to put down instead of Paul R. Smith. I was getting all excited about talking to Mr. Lowe. How would I get him alone? Even Mrs. Lowe can never get hold of Mr. Lowe—he's always out of the country.

I said to Jennie, "Lemme see your list, Star of the East." I tugged her index card from between her fingers. Even Jennie's handwriting has more character than anybody else's. Bold, firm writing, with the straight tails of letters like *y* and *g* slicing down the page. And oh, that first resolution took my mind off Paul in a hurry. For Jennie's first resolution was "Be number three in The Awesome Threesome again." I swallowed hard. Hill and I had ganged up against her. And whose fault was that? It really wasn't Jennie's fault that she had more of the cake, and the best icing, and the thickest filling. Jennie just came that way. No more than it's Paul's fault that his real mother is horrible, his little sister is worse, his father vanished, and his poor stepmother is falling apart. How could one person have so much go wrong in his world? I guess it's no different from Jennie, who has so much go right in her world.

I felt almost soft toward Jennie. But, of course, for Hillary nothing was different. Hill swirled the cooled-off chocolate in her mug. Hill said, "First time you've been willing to be number three, Jennie." Her voice was baiting; there was no friendship in it.

Everybody laughed uneasily.

I looked back down at Jennie's index card. "Two. Win the National Young Composers Contest." Oh, Jennie, I thought. My voice felt queer and frozen. "Three," I read. "Get 800 on my English SATs."

The tearjerker movie was suddenly audible. Its dialogue filled the room, along with the crackle of the fire, and the very faintly heard football commentary from upstairs. It's all right to have wall-to-wall success . . . as long as you stop at one room. But when—tell me, when?—did Jennie ever know enough to stop?

There was a fourth resolution, although Mrs. Lang had said that three were plenty. Jennie, being Jennie, could never stop when anybody else did. "Four," I read, and Hillary's tight face got tighter, and thinner. "Win Paul Classified over."

It made Paul sound like a game. A game Jennie would win because she always had to come in first. Paul—who stayed a secret because he was cracking, not because he was tough.

Jennie, Jennie, I thought. You think Paul is like you: a blazing torch who just happens to avoid the center stage. But he's not. He's cold ashes, he's burned away, there's nothing left now but the sense of duty.

I folded the index card in half to cover up the resolutions. Then I folded it in half again to prevent myself from ripping it up.

"Why don't you add a fifth resolution?" said Hillary, her voice full of rage and pain. "*Show up all my friends* would be a good resolution for you, Jennie," said Hillary. "*Make them look stupid and dull* would be a good resolution for you, Jennie. Of course that's your resolution every day, isn't it, Jennie Quint? You'd better think of a fifth resolution, Jennie Quint, and maybe a sixth because so far it's just the same as last year, Jennie Quint! *Be better than anybody else.*"

Jennie's diary

Skiing makes me hot and sweaty, but the laughter of friends made me warm.

They took me back. The Awesome Threesome existed again. Laughing, jostling, slipping, sliding.

Friends, I thought joyously. We're friends again. After a whole day of thin ice (under the skis and in our conversations) a whole day of feeling as if Emily and Hill were my parole officers—oh, how I loved it! Lying on the rug like old times, Mrs. Lang supervising the fun as if we were still little kids cutting out construction paper.

But in the end I blew it.

I wrote down what I *really* wanted for my resolutions. When will I learn that nobody on this earth wants honesty?

Only ten minutes after I made it, my first resolution failed. "But you weren't serious about wanting the Awesome Threesome to exist anyhow," said Hillary viciously. "And you'd *never* be serious about being *third*, Jennie Quint." Hillary flicked the white index card toward me. It twisted once in the air and fell on the rug by my fingers. "Show-off," said Hillary, in a thin, angry voice.

I choked on the tears, fighting them, almost hitting my eyes with my fists to stop them. "I am *not* a show-off! I just—I'm only—"

But I did not know what to say next. If we took an exam, and I scored lower, I could safely say, "I'm worse than you are." But it's *never* all right to say, "I'm better than you are."

Emily rolled over until she was lying next to Hillary, and I was alone on the far side of the room.

The resolutions literally lay between us.

Paul's diary

At last this so-called vacation is almost over. Used to like vacations. Used to like being home. Used to *have* a home.

Candy came to visit December 26th.

She was there too. *She* had the nerve to tell me I'm acting "immaturely" about this whole thing. I wanted to say, "Hey, I haven't killed you or anything. I think that's very mature of me."

When *she* was gone, I put Candy in the car and we drove to the psychiatric hospital to visit Mom. I can hardly stand to drive in the gates. No place was ever so obviously what this is. A place to stick mental cases you can't handle at home.

Candy was all bubbly about what fun she's having in her new life. What was I supposed to say to my sister? "I'm glad you're having fun, Candy, you've killed Mom, but hey, what's another mother in the debris of life?"

I thought of calling Emily.

I didn't.

I couldn't trust my father or my sister, so what makes me think I could trust anybody else? There isn't anybody to trust.

Maybe not even me.

Mom doesn't trust me.

Every time I visit she looks at me with those starved eyes and doesn't trust me to show up again tomorrow.

Emily's diary

Morning . . . A New Year. And it feels new! New-fallen snow, new moon, new record low. New clothes, almost-new haircut.

New knowledge.

Of me, of friendship, of Paul.

I can't wait to get back to school—see Paul—find out how his mother is doing—be his friend.

Ansley yelled at me for wearing colors that look lousy on me, so for once I took her advice instead of Hill's. I'm going to wear a pale gray cardigan, very oversize (my mother's) with a dark gray and black plaid shirt under it (Ansley's) and earrings in twisted silver ribbons (Ansley's mother's) and gray jeans (mine). In the mirror I look petite and tailored and special.

Oh, this morning, I'm glad to be me!

Paul and I share the secret now, and we'll be friends. And maybe we'll be more than friends.

I'm writing in the car while Hill drives. The Quints pass us. Mrs. Quint drives very fast. Jennie looked into our car and waved. My hand came up to wave back but

Hillary said, "Em, don't start. It's a New Year. Without her."

I thought Hill said, "Without hurt."

Yes.

Let's all have a New Year without hurt.

Evening . . . What good are the perfect clothes if the boy you adore doesn't one single time look in your direction?

Jennie's diary

Fans.

I actually have fans.

Sophomores crowded around me, asking questions, bubbling with the excitement of it all. "We hear you might be getting the pageant published!" they cried. "Is it true?"

Attention is like getting a tan: you feel all hot and glorious. I could bask in it, like summer sun. Of course, as far as Hillary and Emily are concerned, ye season it was winter.

Why is it the strangers who rejoice for me?

Oh, Paul! Paul Classified, why don't you want me? I thought we were two of a kind! I thought when I asked you out, you would sigh with relief, because you need me as much as I need you.

But I was wrong.

You don't need me any more than Hill or Em does.

Of course, my parents rejoice. Smiles of pride wreathe their faces like the green holly on the door. Yesterday I noticed for the first time that my parents don't have any photographs of me framed. Just my writing and artwork and music. What I've *done*. Not what I am.

Dr. Sykes called me out of class. "Report immediately to the office." I thought somebody had been in a car accident, and I raced down to the office, a headache already throbbing.

He wants me to take the examination for Connecticut Star Student. This award is given to twenty students state-wide every year. Our high school is the fourth largest in the state but we haven't had a winner in seven years. You have to have all sorts of academic and activity stuff on your record, but you also have to do very well on an exam they give up in Hartford.

Dr. Sykes (he never says Mr. Sykes, or Jimmy Sykes— it's always Dr. Sykes and he strokes both syllables like a puppy: *Doctor* Sykes) says to me, "Jennie, dear, you have an excellent chance. And it means being on television, being interviewed for *Connecticut Magazine,* being inter-viewed again in the newspapers—that was a lovely article about you and your pageant, my dear—and of course, a fine monetary award for college, which you hardly need, but which will be nice anyhow."

I said, "I thought that only seniors qualified for it."

"No," he said. "Usually it takes four years of high school to compile a track record good enough, but you've been so outstanding you could make it as a junior. Then you'd have a chance of winning *again* as a *senior*—which would be a Connecticut first!"

Oh, how my parents would love that!

Their daughter, a Connecticut first.

But there was one little problem. "Math," I said to Dr. Sykes. "I'm not good at math. I'll score low."

"No problem," he said. "We'll have you tutored."

Ansley's diary

Somebody sent an anonymous letter to Mr. Lowe to ask him to help Paul R. Smith! Mr. Lowe showed us the first sentence to see if we could recognize the handwriting! About the only thing we could say for sure is—it's not Jennie Quint's—her handwriting is too distinctive. Otherwise—it could be anybody's. "Very schoolgirl," said Mr. Lowe thoughtfully.

"What does that mean?" I said.

"Very rounded. Very immature."

Jared and I begged to read the rest of the letter, but Mr. Lowe refused. He said it was in the nature of a confidence between client and lawyer.

"You can't have an anonymous client," said Jared.

Mr. Lowe stared at the contents of the letter. "I rather think I do," he said, and he folded the letter over, and slid it into his breast pocket. Jared and I stared at its white tips, as if it were forbidden fruit.

Mr. Lowe learned some stuff about Paul very quickly—just a few phone calls. When I'm grown up, *my* life will be like that. A few well-placed phone calls to my fascinating friends, and I'll know everything there is to know.

But when we asked what he found out, Mr. Lowe refused to say a single word. "Paul has an unfortunate number of problems. I think I'll have to keep the information classified."

Jared and I laughed until we cried. "You picked the right word, Dad," said Jared.

I've tried diaries before and I give up after about three nights of entries. It's a month now, and I haven't skipped a night. I think it's because of the ordinariness of the notebook. The lovely leather-bound one was no good because my thoughts were too boring to be written on such perfect paper. The Judy Blume one, the Girl Scout one, the five-year one with its little lock and key—they were no good because they were too cute and I felt stupid even opening them. But this plain stenography notebook, with its spiral binding on top, its ugly pages: somehow it's comforting, and welcoming, and a good place to write. I am really getting into this.

I don't like the word "diary." It feels too junior high. I want to call it a journal. More sophisticated, I think.

The journal organizes how I feel about each day.

Was something important enough to write about?

Yes or no?

But of course if it's *really* important, I only *sort of* write about it. The truly truly personal parts I would never write down. I wonder if other people are writing down the really personal things.

The truly personal part today was me and Jared. In place of words, I will use stars. This was a ************ afternoon. Enough written down!

Paul's diary

God, God, God, God, God!

I don't know if I'm swearing or praying.

Maybe it's always that way when I say God's name. Who found out? Who told?

Called to the office—cops there—social worker there—guidance counsellors there—I take one look and I let myself freeze over. They won't reach me. I'm ice.

"You're living alone, Paul," they say. Understandingly. I hate people who try to understand. If I can't understand, how do they dare try? "Boys of sixteen cannot live by themselves," they say. "Now where exactly are your parents?"

I tell them that is not their business. The way my parents and I choose to conduct our lives is private. For a moment this stops them. But only for a moment. The interrogation begins.

What—do they think I murdered my family and buried them in the basement?

At least I know it's not Emily who told, because then they'd know more. They don't even know where my mother is. And if they find out where my father is, I wouldn't mind knowing that myself.

I sit tight, I'm polite, I do nothing. They even call in Miss MacBeth because they know I like her—do they keep little files going?—which teacher does the kid trust? Because we may want a little leverage one day. I smile at

Miss MacBeth because I do like her, but I say nothing. And I know now that no diary of mine gets passed in to anybody.

But something really queer has happened with this diary.

I need it.

If I can't set down what happened in the day I feel like I'm going to suffocate.

It's you and me against the world, book.

Jennie flirted again today.

I held myself back. Easier than it was last time. I have enough energy now for just one person, and if I'm not okay around her, she'll lose it completely.

Jennie's diary

My parents are absolutely thrilled. They can't talk about anything except the Star Student Award. They never heard of it till now, but they don't care about that. They keep hugging me, and laughing to each other, and saying, "Well, it finally paid off, didn't it?"

Like I'm a mortgage.

They're going to burn me to celebrate.

Ansley's diary

Honestly, this school is sick for rumor—I just heard that Jared and I are breaking up! Over Paul Classified!

Well, we were all having lunch—Jared and me and Paul and Keith and Jennie and Emily and Hill—it was egg-salad sandwiches, which I hate, so I was having a lunch of everybody's potato chips and Hillary was lecturing me about nutrition and Jennie was staring wistfully at Paul and Jared said, "So, Ansley Augusta, what's the truth in this?"

I crunched a potato chip very loudly and said, "We've been having a mad affair, haven't we, Paul?"

Paul didn't react at all. I thought he'd make some funny remark and we'd all laugh. But he just sat there. Everybody looked at him. Even Emily, who you would think a person could trust to be sensible, was all gaga over Paul. Honestly, I'd like to locate just one girl who doesn't adore Paul Classified.

"I think there's something wrong with you, P.C.," I said. "Maybe you should go see the school nurse."

Oh, boy, did Jared laugh then. "Ansley, people don't have to see the nurse just because they're not madly in love with you."

I said, "Paul Classified is obviously insane not to take advantage of me. I think the boy needs medication."

Paul roused himself. It took an effort, as if he had fallen into a trance. He said gallantly, "If I could be madly in love, it would be with you, Ansley. Unfortunately, I have no emotions left."

I thought about it all day.

That's his secret.

He has no emotions left. Something drained them all out, and just his body is still there. That's what's classified. Paul is a shell.

Hillary Lang, her journal

It's so boring to make these entries.

I've already told Emily everything, but now I have to set it down on paper as well. Emily says we should run a tape recorder while we talk and then just have my father's secretary transcribe it into our journals. When is this dumb assignment due, anyway? Keeping a diary is a prison sentence.

Jennie's diary

Mother yelled at me because I bit my fingernails down.

I know my hands look awful, but why does every inch of me have to be perfect? I screamed at her, terrible things I never even knew I was thinking! All of a sudden my entire life seemed like walls: huge thick walls of stone that were tumbling in on me, crushing me, pressing my lungs until my ribs poked through. I said, "What difference does it make if my fingernails are ugly?" and she said, "Jennie, I can't bear it when you don't live up to your potential! There's no reason for you to take up nasty habits. Anyway, we're having a party next week."

A party next week.

The best of food, the trendiest of clothing, the most interesting guests—and of course, their best trophy of all: their daughter. Who will be a shinier trophy if her fingernails are long and polished.

I got 89 on my history test for the quarter.

Daddy was bent out of shape because after he read my essay he felt I should have gotten 100. He wanted to call Miss Marcello up and argue with her. I said no, please don't. He said, "How can I brag about an eighty-nine? I like hundreds."

And Mother said dreamily, "Star Student. I like it. My daughter. Gretchen Lowe says in school they're calling you Star of the East, Jennie. Think of it—star of the entire east coast!"

"Mother, they're being sarcastic, and anyway they're referring to the pageant."

My mother never hears the bad things. What I said didn't even pass her earrings, let alone penetrate her brain. "They're so proud of you," she said, beaming.

Right.

Emily's diary

When I knew nothing, I could laugh and shrug and think of other things. Now I think of Paul all day long: does he have enough to eat, is somebody paying the electric bill, how long can he go on like this? I want to ask how his mother is, if he has enough money to put gas in the car to visit her, does he want to come have supper at our house—but he won't look at me.

He's afraid of me.

It makes me feel queasy.

Paul Classified—afraid of me, Emily Weinstein.

Paul, I'm on your team. I really am. Please believe it!

Jennie's diary

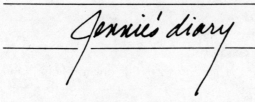

I caught Hill and Emily after school and just climbed into Hill's car so she had no choice but to give me a ride home. I decided just to attack the subject. I said, "Listen. It isn't my fault. I was born this way. It's not fair of you to be jealous."

"Jealous?" said Hillary in this soft, tight voice. "You think one of us is jealous of you, Jennie Quint?"

I ended up apologizing to them. Telling them I'm sorry I said such a terrible thing, and yes, it was very conceited of me, and yes, I'm a very nasty conceited person who deserves to be lonely and friendless.

They didn't say good-bye when I got out of the car, even though I took a long time getting out.

But if they're not jealous—what are they?

What am I?

Emily's diary

I've just figured it out.

Paul Classified has watched The Awesome Threesome die.

He knows I can abandon a friend.

He knows I can plan how to hurt Jennie.

So how can he count on me?

He can't.

Oh, Diary, Diary.

I am afraid of you.

If I did not have to write this down, I could pretend it's not true.

But it is true.

I have not been a friend.

Hillary Lang, her journal

I asked Mom the scary, scary question.

The one I've wanted to ask for two years now.

"Are you jealous, too? Do you want a daughter like Jennie?"

You're not supposed to say things like that out loud. Because what if they're true?

"Not true," said Mom, hugging me hard. "I adore you the way you are." She let go of the hug after a while, and added slowly, almost sadly, "But I guess that nobody can help wanting to glisten and gleam the way Jennie does."

I was really taken aback. "You mean *you* would like to be like Jennie?"

Mom kind of shrugged and laughed at herself. "Sixteen and doing things I haven't done yet at forty? A person can feel old and dumb in a hurry next to Jennie Quint. I wonder how her teachers can stand it."

If Mom felt jealous, too, jealousy seemed almost okay.

"Boy, do I feel good," I said. "Let's go out for dinner. Let's try that new Mexican restaurant on Route One." I was really in the mood for something hot and spicy and demanding. "You know what jealousy looks like?" I asked my mother.

"What?"

"It looks like a rat. Not a cute little white laboratory rat. A hideous evil city slum rat. Biting you."

We both screamed.

Then my mother giggled. "The magazines say you

should have meaningful conversations with your teenager, but I must say a meaningful conversation with you can wipe a mother out, Hill. Let's go out for that Mexican dinner with dad and talk strictly about nonmeaningful things."

I am so lucky to have my mother. What if I had Jennie's mother? Then she'd always be disappointed in me. What could be worse than a mother who doesn't think much of you?

Paul's diary

This Mr. Lowe shows up out of nowhere, saying he's got a son my age and he wants to help.

I know he has a son my age. He has a son my age I despise from the bottom of my heart. (Such as my heart is.)

And you know—I almost did talk.

I wanted to talk so bad it was like starvation. I could taste it. I had a hard time breathing. Made me think of Jennie, and how her lungs collapse when she laughs. Great, I thought, I'm having a nervous breakdown. Two in one family. Wonderful success rate at coping.

"Why not talk?" said Mr. Lowe.

I actually answered him. I said, "I might burst."

Mr. Lowe is rather heavy, not as tall as I am, wearing a dark suit and a heavy city-type coat. He doesn't look one bit like Jared. Jared is thin and preppy, Mr. Lowe is old and tired. And in his speech, he pauses, just the way I do, thinking before he says anything out loud. "Like a dam?" he said slowly. "Too much pressure behind it?"

But I had already said too much. I didn't add to it.

Mr. Lowe was looking at my sleeves. It was a parent look. Good grief, does this mean I have to get you yet another wardrobe? Didn't I just buy you all new clothes? When are you going to stop growing? My mother used to say things like that all the time, but laughing, and then Candy and I would back up against the wall in our last house, and measure how much we'd grown, and when Dad came home, we'd show him how high the new marks were.

I looked at Mr. Lowe's shoes. Expensive, shiny shoes that commuters wear, not high-school kids. I'm down to one pair: high-tops I'm going to have to slit the toes on before long.

"I'd like you to live with us, Paul," said Mr. Lowe. "Until things are straightened out."

Me? Live with Little Yuppie Jared? Watch the Prep Couple of the Decade on their pin-striped couch together? Me—drive around in Jared's little red Porsche, and help him fasten his little Rolex on his wrist?

I walked away from Mr. Lowe.

He's a little more gracious than his son. He didn't follow me.

Ansley's diary

The school is providing Jennie Quint with a special tutor for the math section of the Star Student Examination. I could spit. Where do they get off, grooming her like some gymnastics star for the Olympics? Jennie's family has tons of money, they can afford their own tutor! I absolutely cannot stand it that the school has already decided Jennie deserves more than the rest of us. I wanted to organize a protest, but everybody else said No, let Jennie hang herself. It's about time anyway.

JARED'S DIARY

Even I could not believe it, and I am definitely used to Jennie by now.

I rank seventeenth in a class of 310, and I'm pretty involved. I'm the diving team captain and associate editor of the monthly paper. I've been in charge of the student Bloodmobile and the Student Art Museum.

We get back from vacation, pretty much ready to be nice and kind and generous of heart—you know, all that Christmas stuff—and there's Dr. Sykes telling the entire school that junior Jennie Quint is going to outclass every senior and every junior in the state of Connecticut, and set records, and be her own display case in the lobby.

Jennie didn't look at anybody else when the announcement came over the loudspeaker. I guess she figured there was nobody worth looking at.

"If there were letters for academic and musical achievement," said Dr. Sykes, "we would retire Jennie Quint's number!"

I've never been mad at Jennie for being Jennie.

I've always been proud of me for being me.

But where do they get off—making Jennie so special? And where does *she* get off—doing it?

And in every single class I share with Jennie, the teachers announce their pride in her! In English, in physics, the teacher stands up and says proudly, "Isn't it exciting?"

No.

It isn't exciting.

Every single kid here would like to kick Jennie Quint in the shins.

Ansley's diary

The cafeteria was a mob again. Very different from the mob Paul faced. This was a mob against Jennie, and it was verbal, not physical, and it was girls, not boys.

I could feel the mob forming and I just stayed out of it.

I didn't want to be part of that again.

The top seniors are absolutely seething with rage. Going up to Hartford for two days for Star Student is a real prize. They take you out of class—it's a Thursday and Friday, and you stay at the Sheraton, and you're with another 150 of the finest Connecticut has to offer, and you put this on your college applications, and all—and a junior is going to outshine them. They know perfectly well they can't win against Jennie.

Amanda Hodges was maddest of all. "This is for seniors," she snaps. Amanda is first in the class, but that's all she does. She can't win and we all know it. Amanda's never even *met* the other kids in the class, let alone worked with them—she's always home studying. "But when I went in to Dr. Sykes to complain, do you know what he said to me, Jennie Quint?"

Jennie stared at her without speaking.

"Dr. Sykes explained to me that dear Jennie is very precocious." Her voice was thin and enraged and sliced across the room. Jennie flinched as if Amanda's voice had actually hit her. "The school system, he explained to me, makes exceptions for quality students." Amanda's hatred could have been put on a plate and served. I suppose normal cafeteria food would taste pretty terrific after a portion of Amanda's jealousy.

Jennie was pale and shaken. "Star Student wasn't my idea," she protested.

"Fine," said Amanda. "Then why don't you wait 'til next year? Several of us in the senior class have an excellent chance, and you know that each high school can have only one winner."

Paul Classified looked at me and said, "I don't know how to rescue her." I said, "She'll have to rescue herself, Paul. The only thing she can do is agree to drop out of the running."

102

Jennie was thinking about it—you could tell—but Amanda went wrong. Raising her voice so that nobody in the entire cafeteria could possibly not hear, she said, "*We're* just plain old ordinary seniors. *Jennie,* of course, is *special.* How stupid of us to think *we* could be special when *Jennie* is around."

Jennie's chin tilted up and I knew right away that Amanda's tactics were wrong. Attacking Jennie in public was dumb; Jennie wouldn't be defeated in front of us. She would rather be dead.

"The rest of us are only around for show," said Amanda fiercely. "Dr. Sykes believes you have it all sewn up."

Jennie stood up and narrowed her eyes. Very softly, Jennie said, "Amanda, we're all taking the same examinations, and we all fill out the same applications. Either you're a star student or you're not."

Paul whistled.

I sighed.

It was going to be war now.

And I know Jennie doesn't want war. She wants friends.

Well, she chose it. She can't pretend otherwise.

Jennie's diary

Paul Classified is just the only one who admits it.

All of us keep our thoughts classified.

I have a cat at home. Isabelle. Once I had Ferdinand

and Columbus to go with Isabelle, but Ferdinand ran away and Columbus preferred living at Hillary's house. Hillary calls Columbus "Cat," and Cat comes whenever Hill yells for him. Isabelle doesn't have a hard time being a cat. You never see Isabelle lying awake all night biting her nails fretting about being a cat. But people—we spend half our lives figuring out how to be what we were born being.

We are the only species that has a hard time being a species.

Perhaps that's why we are willing to write these diaries.

We're trying to declassify ourselves.

I do not have a friend in the world now.

It's this math tutoring.

I don't know how to get out of it.

I told my parents and I told Dr. Sykes it wouldn't work out.

But they think I'm just succumbing to peer pressure. That's actually what they said to me. I tell them the entire school is mad at me over this Star Student thing and I want to pull out and they say, "Jennie, dear, don't succumb to peer pressure."

Peer pressure!

What a stupid, stupid, stupid, stupid, stupid phrase.

They are my friends, my world, my life, and they hate me.

That's not peer pressure.

That's suicide.

Oh, I don't know what to do, I hurt so much, *I hurt so much!*

Paul's diary

It was war there for a while and I thought of joining Jennie's team, but she didn't look my way. She stared her enemies straight in the eye and she refused to surrender. I couldn't just walk over to her; she didn't want me. Ansley and I talked about it. Jennie's made her first really major mistake, I think. You can outshine everybody only so long, and then you have to blend in with the crowd. Now they're going to turn on her.

It makes me sick, but I don't know how to help her. Amanda Hodges doesn't lay off.

When we were going back to class after lunch, and I was trying to catch up to Jennie to tell her I was on her team, Amanda said something I couldn't catch to Jennie. It must have been some blackmail, because Jennie said, "All right, I'll go tell Dr. Sykes I'm going to withdraw." She looked confused and unpoised for the first time I can ever remember.

But Dr. Sykes was coming down the hall, and Sykes had no idea that anything other than his school's record was at stake. He was terribly upset. "This is my high school's chance to set yet another record!" he cried. "Think of the trophies you'll bring home! Why, Jennie, the front lobby will have the Star Student award for two years running! We'll all be so proud of it."

"Of it?" said Jennie. "Of *it?*" She was actually shaking, and then she laughed hysterically. "They bagged me in Africa, you know," she said crazily.

It was not like Jennie to be weird. Everybody just looked at her.

Jennie turned to Amanda. "Or you could polish me," she said, going on down the hall. "I might be silver. I might be gold."

Candy used to sing a song about silver and gold in Brownie Scouts. Make new friends, but keep the old, one is silver and the other gold.

But Ansley thought she was referring to the trophies in the front foyer. You can polish trophies.

Jennie, bagged in Africa? Silver and gold?

For an entire half day, Jennie was the mystery, and not me.

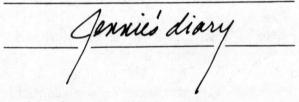

Jennie's diary

I wanted something to hurt me.

It was so weird.

I had an evening rehearsal at school, and when it ended, I didn't catch a ride with anybody and I didn't call my mother. I just started walking.

I didn't button my coat, wanting the wind to freeze me. I didn't zip my pocketbook, wanting the money and the credit cards to fall out. I didn't walk in the sunlight, but late at night, downtown, in dark shadows past littered gutters. I chose neighborhoods where crime is heavy and violent.

But nothing happened.

And in the end I came out at the corner of High Street and Ridge Road, and who pulled up next to me? Paul Classified. "Get in, Jennie," he said. "I'll give you a ride home. What are you doing walking around at this hour?"

I walk in places where I could get mugged and raped, and what happens? I end up just where I've wanted to be all along: Paul Classified's car.

The night was extraordinarily dark—cloudy, with no moon. Leaves flickered across the pavement like scurrying animals; I kept thinking we were going to run over a squirrel. We were trapped in the car together for the eleven miles to my house.

Paul said, "Had a pretty tough day in school, didn't you?" He drove very well: hard, as if the sharp curves of narrow Connecticut roads were a test of life.

"Every day is a tough day now."

He was staring straight ahead. His features were so clean in profile, like something that should be on a gold coin—something you could outline with a pen and frame. Paul said, "Do you need to talk?"

Oh, but there were so many problems. I didn't even know how to start. How could I have turned a whole school against me just because I'm good? I had to fight sobs. Oh, how I wanted Paul to care about me. I wanted him to touch me, or hug me. I felt like a little kid with a skinned knee: somebody please put a Band-Aid on my cut!

"I'm listening," said Paul a mile later.

"Emily and Hill are jealous." Better for once to start small than my usual technique of starting impressive.

"I know."

"They're my best friends."

Paul nodded. "It hurts them that you succeed left and

right hardly trying, and they muddle along behind you."

He was on their side, too. He didn't care that it hurt me—only that it hurt them!

"Stay out of those neighborhoods," he said suddenly. "You're playing with fire."

"Do you care?"

Paul Classified stared at me, his face blank. "I have gone out of the business of caring. Don't expect caring from me, Jennie."

"Why?"

"I have no emotion to spare. I'm using it for something else. I go to school for an education, and that's that. Not for friends or fun."

"Oh, Paul! That's terrible. Education is the least of the things you go to school for! Friends and fun are higher up!"

Paul actually laughed out loud. "You don't really think that, Jennie. You who have to succeed or die trying. You read that in a magazine somewhere. It has nothing to do with your life."

"Success doesn't matter that much to me."

"Oh no? I think, Jennie, that you would give up almost anything in order to succeed. Including Emily and Hill."

"They're giving me up!"

"So fail a little," said Paul. "They'd come back then."

To fail, I would have to fail on purpose. Say to myself: Now I will write a stupid paper; now I will figure out the wrong answers on the quiz; now I will forget the melody to my own song. "*Fail?*"

"Scary word, huh?"

I guess it must be, because I leaped away from failure and I said to him, "So what is this huge problem that uses up all your emotion, Paul?"

He said nothing.

We turned up Talcott Hill.

"Answer me. It's the courteous thing."

"I'm giving you a ride home, lady. Taking myself miles out of my way for you. The courteous thing is not to interrogate me."

"Oh," I said. "Sorry about that."

Unexpectedly he took his eyes off the road to smile at me. A smile to be cherished, because it was infrequent: like getting a compliment from a teacher who rarely gives A's. "Jennie," he said, "your timing isn't so good. Just trust me. We all have problems. Some of us can only deal with them in silence."

Oh, how I wanted to know more! "I'll help!" I said. "Is it money or family or alcohol or drugs or prison or illegal aliens? Tell me! Let me be part of it!"

"No," said Paul Classified.

The wind caught on the whip of an antenna and screamed as the car turned up Talcott Hill.

"Here's your house, Jennie." He sat very still behind the wheel, neither looking at me nor reaching toward me. I knew that if I flung myself on him he would still just sit there, staying out of it. He won't let me in his life, and he won't come into mine. He leaned over me, but did not touch me, and opened my door. Cold wind brushed over us both, but it was the only thing we shared.

I went in the house. He waited to be sure I got in safely. How crazy life is. On Lost Pond Road, where everything ends happily ever after, cushioned by money and style, he waits to be sure I'm safe.

Paul's diary

I drive at night. I can't sit in the darkness alone at home. Funny how I still call it home when it's just a place where my clothes are in drawers. Found Jennie Quint of all people wandering around a slum.

I worry about her. I will explode from the inside: secrets will burst my skin. But Jennie will explode from the outside: pressure will detonate her control.

And what will she do when she explodes? I'm different: I have a mother to visit. But Jennie has to get *away* from her parents! Or maybe away from herself.

Where will she go? Can she wait for college: one and a half years? A girl walking alone in the freezing dark is not in a waiting mood.

Success.

Jennie's success is going to tear her to pieces.

Me, if I could succeed in just one thing, I'd be so happy. All I want to do is be sure Mom knows she's my mother. Candy's gone. It's as if Mom had never tucked her in at night, or read her stories, or been her Brownie Scout leader, or fixed her banana milkshakes. It's all on me. I have to be a great son from now on, because Mom is counting on me to be the child she succeeds with.

I guess the real definition of love is that there are no conditions. They love you no matter what. I love Mom no matter what.

But nobody loves Jennie no matter what. People love

her because she's brilliant and exciting. Even her mother and father . . .

I didn't know a diary would be like this.

I didn't know that all day long part of my mind would sift through my thoughts choosing the ones I would write down.

Miss MacBeth, are you safe? I watch you now, in class, weighing you. I am pretty sure now I will never pass this in. I'll get an F. But I don't have a mother anymore who either knows or cares. Jennie's parents would kill her for getting an F. They'd probably kill her for getting an A minus.

Or am I wrong? After all, her parents aren't doing all this composing and writing and test taking—Jennie is.

Maybe Jennie would kill *herself* for getting an A minus.

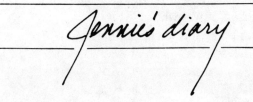

Jennie's diary

Snow days.

Oh, magic!

No school!

White, cold, shivery freedom.

In the old days, The Awesome Threesome was at its best on a snow day. Snowmen and sleds and skis.

I was sitting in my bedroom, staring down at the meadows and woods and hills of Lost Pond Road, thinking how gloriously beautiful it was in the first snow of winter.

And I truly thought—I'm not kidding you—I am not lying—I am not exaggerating—I am not trying to cover for myself! I truly thought those two men were some horrible gang, coming to rob or rape or vandalize. The roar of the snowmobiles was like the hill opening up, and the stones screaming.

Nobody around here has a snowmobile. We use skis. We don't desecrate the serenity of Lost Pond with screaming, screeching snowmobiles. They sound like a gang of berserk chainsaws committing murder.

And those men—they were dressed all in black. Black boots, black jackets, black pants, black gloves, black helmets.

Naturally I ran down to rescue Hillary and Emily. (And, I suppose, rescue our friendship while I was at it.)

Well, okay.

It was an error.

A major error.

But it seemed reasonable at the time.

I guess that's how it is with all major errors.

"Ye season, it was winter."

Oh is it ever. And me frozen out.

Emily's diary

They swung their snowmobiles in tight screaming circles. What a turn on! Literally! Scott twisted in two circles coming down the hill in our backyard, and Brandon fishtailed, and then they circled Hillary and me, and we were laughing and thinking—two boys! And two of us! Now that's arithmetic!

Scott had filled out. All the boys do, between ninth and eleventh grade, but you forget just how much filling out is involved. Scott's over six feet, and still thin, but now the thin isn't junior-high scrawny: it's senior-high lithe and athletic. He got a buzz a while ago, and it's somewhat grown out: light brown bristles curling in places, and straight up in the air in others. I had to stifle an impulse to flatten it down with my hand. He no longer wore glasses: probably had contacts. His complexion was dark because he needed to shave.

Wow! If that's what prep school does for boys, they should all go.

Oh, I hate Jennie Quint.

She did it on purpose.

She sat up there at that window of hers, and she couldn't stand it that Hillary and I might have something she didn't have.

Ansley's diary

My new ski outfit is mauve. I love it. And my day was perfect until two snowmobiles, huge screaming black models, like Harley-Davidson motorcycles without wheels, shrieked across the snow and cut through the top of Jennie's land.

Snowmobiles are for people who are lazy and out of shape and hate nature. Nobody on Lost Pond Lane would ever think of owning one. Whoever rode that snowmobile over Talcott Hill was trespassing, ruining the peacefulness of our road with that garbage.

But I certainly knew who it was.

And Emily and Hillary certainly knew.

Look how fast they waltzed out into the snow and stood there so nobody could miss them posing.

I said to Jared, "Two boys at a time. Even for Jennie Quint, that is conspicuous consumption."

"What's conspicuous consumption?" said Jared.

"You retard. We just learned about it in economics. Having too much just to show off by."

Jared laughed. "That's not just Jennie. That's everybody on Lost Pond Road."

Paul's diary

Snow days. The whole town is out skiing and skating and making snowmen and tearing around on snowmobiles. We used to do that. Mom and I. Dad and I. Candy and Mom and Dad and I.

I thought I would stay Classified and have only the problems of Mom and Dad and Candy to deal with. (Only?)

But there are more!

There's Emily—I owe her a debt, and I can't seem to do anything about it.

There's Mr. Lowe—he's written me a letter and enclosed some cash. I spent it, which obviously means I accepted it, and now I have a debt there, too. And an extra debt, because Jared and Ansley obviously know nothing about it.

And there's Jennie. Who would kill herself over an A minus.

Would she really?

Those girls ganging up on her? Losing Emily and Hillary? Wandering around a slum at night? Getting weird talking about silver and gold?

Jennie I should help.

How crazy. The boy who has nothing thinking about helping the girl who has everything.

Hillary Lang, her journal

Me, naturally, I'm wearing Aunt Vicki's old coat with the rips, and Emily's little brother Trip's scarf he usually uses on snowmen. Because I wasn't going anywhere except Em's. Jennie, naturally, she's flung her mother's new scarlet cloak over her shoulders, so she looks romantic, and snowy, and feminine, and perfect.

"Jennie!" says this so-called threatening robber. "It's only been two years and you don't recognize me? I guess that's what happens when you're famous. You develop a whole new circle of friends and don't talk to the old ones."

"Scott van Elsen," says Jennie, laughing. "I thought you were a fierce robber trespassing on Lost Pond Lane." She gives him a hug. "Oh, Scott, you look simply wonderful. Of course, attack black is not your best color."

"Looks good against the snow," Scott tells her. And

then, as if Emily and I are not standing there, he performs introductions. "Jennie, I'd like you to meet my roommate, Brandon. Brandon, this is the famous composer, musician, lyricist, and scholar my mother was telling us about. We missed your pageant, Jennie, but I hear from my mother it's going to be published."

Jennie laughs gaily, flirting a mile a minute. She doesn't say hello to us. She doesn't even pretend to notice us. In fact, I don't think she *did* notice us. "Your mother heard that from my mother. My mother would like to have it published, but so far it's all in her head." Now she starts flirting with Brandon, who is not half as good-looking as Scott. Maybe not a third as good-looking. Ten percent on a good day. "I'm from Georgia," said Brandon. "I'm used to snow now that I've been at the Academy for three years, but this is my first time on a snowmobile."

Listen, there's no snow on Jennie. Quick as an ice storm, she cries, "I've never ridden on one myself." Never mind that she wouldn't be caught dead on a snowmobile, that we all hate them, that people with snowmobiles should be shot. Jennie bats her eyes, and sure enough, "But you've got to try mine, Jennie," cries Scott, right on cue, as if Jennie had handed him the script of her life, "and then you'll change your mind. We'll see the woods the way you never have. Put away that ritzy uptown jacket and I'll take you out."

If looks could kill, Jennie would be embalmed. *Now* she turns to us and says, "Hi." She swallows, like she doesn't know how to keep her boyfriends and have her friendships too. I'm not surprised. I don't know how she's going to do it, either.

She says, "How are you?"

I say, "Oh, we're quite well, thank you, Jennie."

Scott is laughing at us.

Even when she's being rotten, Jennie wins! Scott thinks *I* am funny because I'm jealous, and Jennie comes out smelling like a rose because she's not jealous!

"A little New England hostility here, Brandon," says Scott, revving his motor and following Miss Quint. "Kind of the opposite of southern hospitality, you know what I mean?"

Brandon must know, because he goes after Scott, ignoring us, and Jennie has two boys for the day.

Some snow day.

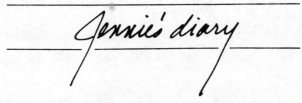

So I'm on a snowmobile for the first time, vibrating all over from the engine, my legs straddling Scott, his warmth soaking through me.

I am thinking of Emily's face, and Hillary's eyes, and I am afraid ever to come back down Talcott Hill.

How could I have done that?

I was terrible, I was awful, and every moment when I could have stopped myself, I didn't.

It's because I'm so mad at them both!

It isn't my fault I'm smarter than they are! If they can't flirt right with Scott and Brandon, that's their fault! I tell myself, louder than the motors on the snowmobiles.

But I'm lying. I was getting back at them. I don't care one whit about Scott or Brandon or their entire prep school of male bodies. I wanted to smack Hillary and Emily as hard as they've smacked me all year.

We skirted the old stone walls to find breaks. We came out at Burying Hill, which I didn't even know you could get to from Lost Pond. The roar of the motors was like a great crashing chord that didn't stop.

We went to the very top of Burying Hill, the thick snow welcoming us, slipping through thickets that would be impenetrable in spring. Scott turned off the engine. Brandon swerved up, slid in the snow, and turned his off, too.

In the sudden silence, I looked down on the valley as the first settlers must have known it. *Ye Season It Was Winter.* A sonnet to snow formed in my mind: beaten down by the elements, and yet worshipful. Reverent before God and nature.

Scott said, "What are you doing this weekend, Jennie? Want to go into the city with Brandon and me?"

Emily's diary

Well, there were three of us again. But this time the third was Ansley, and we were definitely not awesome. We were *awful.*

Basketball season, right?

We're having a reasonably good year, which considering it's Westerly High is absolutely amazing. We do stuff like ski team, fencing team, soccer team, and diving team, but we don't exactly shine in basketball.

Still, everybody basically likes basketball, so there we all were, in the gym, at night, yelling our heads off.

Ansley is without Jared. She says this in a way that

makes you think she's without arms, or hair. "He'll be here later," she says carelessly. "We just couldn't manage all the cars tonight, what with everybody going in different directions." Ansley frowns a little tiny frown to match her little tiny mind. She said, "Having a boyfriend really makes life complex, you know."

We should all have that complexity in life.

In comes Jennie. She pauses at the door of the gym, and looks across the bleachers. It's that *where do I sit?* look. Remember—from junior high, when you were so afraid you'd have nobody to sit with? And you didn't even go places unless you already had somebody? I suddenly realized that was one reason The Awesome Threesome existed to start with—that way, we would never be alone. Everybody would know we were popular.

I stared at Jennie, alone in the gym door. We were packed into the fourth bleacher up. There was not a single space . . . unless, of course, we picked up all our coats, and piled them somewhere else, and squished over, and let Jennie in.

Jennie walked toward us. She was nervous. You could tell.

Hillary looked at me. Everybody else looked at both of us. Would we be loyal to our best friend and give her space? Or would we stare at her and let her be alone?

Keith Malone, one of the seniors who are eligible for Star Student application, leaned between Hill and me and said very loudly, "If it isn't the Star of the East! Look at that! Somebody lend me sunglasses, I can hardly see! She's shining so brightly!"

Be loyal! I thought. Stand up for her!

But I didn't. I didn't say a single word. I braided the tassels on the end of my scarlet and white scarf.

And Keith said, "So how's that math tutoring going,

Miss Quint? You reach perfection yet? We wouldn't want you to settle for anything less."

Ansley said, "Lay off, Malone."

Jennie was standing right in front of us. She smiled her usual bright smile and said, "I'm a little worried about the math, to tell the truth."

Keith gasped loudly. "Worried? Jennie Quint? Oh, Jennie, we wouldn't want that! You must scurry to Dr. Sykes and he'll help you."

Jennie's chin tipped up and her cheeks went red.

Amanda Hodges said, "But she's just a little worried, Keith. Jennie would never worry *much*."

I looked up. Jennie was waiting for me. She still expected friendship from me—after all these snubs, she still thought I would come through and be nice to her. I muttered, "Hillary, shove over and let her in."

Hillary said, "No, Em, forget it. We're too crowded."

Jennie whirled away, running back toward the door of the gym.

I almost jumped over the three rows below me and ran after her. "Hill, we can't do this to her."

"Oh, Emily," said Hillary angrily, "you were the one who was the most jealous."

"I know, but I wasn't the most mean."

"Mean*est*, dummy," said Amanda Hodges.

I grabbed my coat to go after her and haul her back when in the door came Scott and Brandon. Handsome, overdressed, amused by the whole place. They said, "Jennie! Great! We were hoping to run into you! We're slumming, going to a public-school game! Want to sit with us?"

Keith Malone said, "Slumming?"

Amanda Hodges said, "It is Jennie, Keith dear. She's far superior to the common run of Westerly students, you know."

120

Jennie didn't look back. She crossed the gym and sat opposite us, Scott on her left and Brandon on her right.

I would feel guilty and awful and rotten through and through (in fact, I *do* feel guilty and awful and rotten through and through), but Jennie coming out on top again just made me weary. So I didn't call her up to apologize, and after the game Hill and I stood around joking with Jared and Ansley so we wouldn't have to talk to Jennie and Brandon and Scott in the front foyer.

This is getting bad.

I am going downhill faster than on skis.

Hillary Lang, her journal

Jennie gets Scott and Brandon. How does she do it? Anybody else would have dragged home with her tail between her legs, utterly miserable and defeated. Jennie ends up with two handsome rich boys. I have never known a single person in my life who so consistently ends up better off than the rest of us.

So far we hadn't glanced at the game yet, and it wouldn't be any time soon that we did, because Paul Classified appeared in the doorway to the gym. From everywhere, girls' eyes drifted toward him and locked.

Paul was wearing jeans, and a fleece-lined jeans jacket. He had a hard look to him, as if it would be dangerous to talk to him. He needed a haircut. That thick dark brown hair was in his eyes. Very slowly Paul Classified pushed it back. You could hear this female group sigh. Paul Classified didn't notice; the basketball teams didn't notice; maybe the parents didn't notice. Jennie Quint noticed. She stood up and waved at Paul.

Paul had never come to a game before that I knew of. I wanted him to sit with me—or us, rather—but if the choice was Jennie or elsewhere, I wanted him to sit with boys, who would welcome him because Paul had their respect, but he wouldn't really be one of them: he'd be with them.

Sit with me, sit with me! I thought at him, willing him to pick me out of the crowd. Paul circled the gym and climbed up to sit with Jennie Quint, who already had Brandon on her left and Scott on her right.

You should have heard us then.

Now I know that lightning does *not* strike when you say bad things, because lightning didn't strike and if anybody ever deserved it, we did. We were horrible, we spent the whole basketball game saying terrible things about Jennie Quint.

I kept thinking—Jennie and I were best friends. We did everything together. Which of us is bad right this minute? Me or Jennie?

Oh, I don't want to keep a diary anymore! Putting these thoughts on paper makes me feel so much worse. I can't pretend I'm good when I see them written down.

I'm not writing stuff like this anymore.

After this, I'm writing strictly facts. Weather, headlines, and homework.

No more truth.

The end.

Love, Hillary . . . (although I should invent a new way of signing off, because right now I certainly don't feel loving. So I'll write—)

Anger, Hillary

JARED'S DIARY

Well, old P.C. definitely is a mystery after all.

Last week in school (where I figured it was a little safer) I apologized to him for following him. He said nothing, of course. His face just froze over as if it were water in January. What he was mostly doing was not decking me. Then he walked away. How can somebody who says so little, moves so little, does so little—reduce me to nothing so thoroughly?

So just when I knew where I stood (in danger), he started being friendly to me. A mere few weeks after I thought he was going to strangle me right out on the highway. In fact, the way he looks at me, you'd think *I'm* the mystery.

At least I don't have to worry about being attacked. And Paul doesn't have to worry about being followed. I think he taught me a minor lesson.

During the basketball game not one girl saw a single point being made. They spent the entire game talking about how Jennie Quint has gotten Paul. Forget it. Paul doesn't even know Jennie's there. He's just staying safe, with a pair of strangers: Brandon and Scott he'll never see again in his life.

Jennie's diary

Paper. I cannot believe that the only friend I have is a piece of paper. Nobody else to listen to me? Nobody else to tell things to?

I don't want to be sitting home writing my triumphs down in some lousy stenographer's notebook!

I want to be at McDonald's having a strawberry shake with Emily and Hillary. I want to be at school throwing the whipped cream on top of the Jell-O at Ansley. I want to be telling Paul, or Keith, or Jonathan, or Brian, or Matthew. . . .

I am telling my diary.

Like a sixth grader who just moved to a new town.

Dear Diary, you'll have to be my friend because I don't know anybody else. Oh, how pitiful.

And it's me.

Brandon and Scott. Those girls who were so jealous of me should have been there. It wasn't a date, just a row of three. Nobody held hands. Nobody kissed. Nobody uttered a single personal syllable. The boys talked about cars and engines and good buys in electronic equipment.

Anyway, I wanted to be with Paul Classified, not Scott and Brandon. I know—I just *know*—that if I got to know Paul better he would be exciting. His little sister Candy—it could be anything. From illegal adoption to early childhood drug addiction, you know?

Actually when I waved at Paul to come sit with us, I was rather hoping he would get jealous himself. He might think, I don't want Jennie running around with these other guys from the Yuppie Yard. I want her for myself. And he'd ask me out!

Well, he sat with us, but he sat next to Scott and they talked through the entire basketball game about snowmobiles, because Paul used to have one.

I couldn't even see Paul very well. I spent most of the game watching Hillary and Emily laughing. How long has it been since I laughed like that? I used to laugh all the time.

Mother is having a big party Sunday night. Forty guests. It's a Celebrate the Star Student party. I said, "But Mother, I haven't even gone to Hartford to take the examinations yet." She just laughed and kissed me and went on dialing the caterer. "You'll win, dear," she said confidently. "Daddy and I have absolute trust in your brains and ability."

JARED'S DIARY

We had a very unexpected dinner guest . . . Paul Classified.

Ansley and I got home from working on our term papers at the library and Dad drove in the driveway and he had P.C. with him.

It was the most awkward dinner of my entire life. Paul hates me because I follow him around. Ansley likes Paul more than I want her to. My father knows everything

125

about Paul and won't tell me any of it. And Mother, she never notices anything amiss, she just tells all these incredibly boring stories about contractors who didn't show up to work on the addition, or how sweet the man at the dry cleaner's was to her.

Paul liked my mother, which made me think that I needed binoculars to see Paul better.

When I drove Ansley home, she said, "Well, that was weird."

I said, "I have the impression my father is adopting another son."

Ansley said, "Or maybe your mother is. They were really interested in Paul."

"I didn't pick up any clues, though, did you?"

Ansley hadn't learned anything more about P.C. either, but she told me about his middle name—Paul Revere and all that stuff. I was furious! She knew all these weeks and didn't tell me? "It was private," she said, as if she was surprised that it mattered to me.

All the world has something private going on with Paul Classified.

I went straight home, and Dad had taken Paul back to wherever Paul lives, and I demanded explanations.

Zip.

My father shrugged.

I yelled, "Dad! You can't shrug! I'm your son! Tell me what's going on!"

"Can't."

My mother said, "Jared, darling, one of these days Paul will open up and talk about it, but until then, play along, all right?"

Now I was really outraged. "You know all about Paul too?" I demanded. "The two of you are taking Paul on as a cause or something?"

My mother put her hands on my cheeks and said, "Sweetie, this is a test. I'll be proud of you for taking Paul on yourself, and asking no questions until he's ready to talk."

Now what do you say when your mother comes on like that? Naturally you have to say, "Yes, Mother, I'll ace the test, you'll be proud of me."

When she left the room I said, "Come on, Dad, satisfy my curiosity," and he said, "No."

That's the trouble with having a lawyer in the family: all these one-syllable dead ends.

JARED'S DIARY

The whole school is against Jennie.

You can feel it, like the excitement before a big game: it's the excitement of seeing Jennie lose.

It's sick.

Reminds me of that day when the guys attacked Paul Classified in the cafeteria.

I try to figure out what Jennie's crime is. Not that she was born brilliant and beautiful and rich—Ansley's all of that and nobody hates Ansley. It's that Jennie *works so hard*. We don't mind brains if you just let the brains sit around. But when you fling yourself into it, when you have ten times the energy of everybody around you, we get mad at you. You're showing us up.

If Jennie wins Star Student, she's lost all of us.

If Jennie loses Star Student, she's still lost all of us.

She's going to be the greatest winner this school ever saw . . . and the biggest loser.

Jennie's diary

It's dark now, and quiet, and very, very late, although I can't see my clock because I'm huddling under the covers. I'm trying to decide something. If I fail, will I get Emily and Hillary back? If I say, "You're right, I'm not that good"—will they like me again? Or have I blown it forever? Suppose I become ordinary, like Em and Hill? Suppose I stopped composing *Ye Season, It Was Winter?* Suppose I skipped assignments, and didn't pass in term papers, and got C's and D's, and maybe dropped my music classes, and stayed out of drama club? Would they take me back?

I don't think so.

I think they would say, "You're doing it on purpose, Jennie, and so it doesn't count."

I think they would say, "You're doing it just to get more attention, Jennie, and so we don't care."

I think there's no way I can ever have a friend again.

My success killed them.

My success will kill me, too.

Why aren't you proud of me? I'm doing my best! Why isn't that good? Why is that bad?

I'm sorry, okay? I didn't mean to be good. I'm not this way in order to ruin your chances. I was born this way, you guys!

I wonder what the other winners of Star Student have been like. Did they have friends? Were they able to pull off success without people hating them?

But what if I've spent all this year blaming this on being too good for my own good . . . and what if it really is me? What if I really am a bad person?

Paul's diary

I couldn't go to school.

I went to the hospital to see her.

She was asleep.

I didn't know what to do, so I just sat in the lobby. I sat there for a long time, holding an old *Time* magazine in my lap and staring at the window of the gift shop. If I had money I could buy my mother a pretty gown. Or a paperback book.

A long time passed, and I didn't move. There was no place to move to.

Jared Lowe's father sat down next to me. He said hello. I didn't say anything. He said, "Paul, I have a good life, a soft life. You have a bad life, a hard life, a life of rocks and sharp edges. But one way to have an easier life is to let other people help you. Nobody can go it alone. When your father abandoned you, because the going got too rough for him, you and your stepmother tried to go it alone. And it didn't work. You both completely fell apart."

"I did not fall apart," I said.

"Yes, you did. It just doesn't show as much on you as

it does on your mother." He put his arm around my shoulder. For a minute it was just there, and then he tightened it around me in a little hug.

This is it, I thought, the moment I've been afraid of for a year now: I'm going to collapse, the dam is breaking.

Mr. Lowe said, "You don't have to talk. All you have to do is let me buy you a hamburger."

I kind of laughed. I said, "I am pretty hungry."

Mr. Lowe said, "Maybe two hamburgers."

And I said, "The thing is, I don't even like Jared."

"You grew up years ahead of him, Paul. He'll get there eventually. I kind of enjoy him myself."

I said, "You're his father. You ought to."

Mr. Lowe said, "I'd like to be your temporary father, if you'd allow that."

February

Paul's diary

Temporary father.
But that's suitable, I suppose.
All my parents have been temporary.
I cannot believe I am living with the Lowes. But what choice was there? And I admit to a diary only, I was too tired to argue.

Jennie's diary

Nobody wished me luck.
Nobody asked me if I felt okay, or was nervous, or had studied for it. They all just looked at me, with mocking cruel looks, hoping I would fail. Well, I won't fail! I don't care what anybody thinks, I don't care how lonely I am, I will succeed, just as I always succeed, and Mother and Daddy will be proud.
They hired a bus to take the seniors and me to the state capital. Not your usual uncomfortable yellow school

133

bus, but a plush travel bus with a bathroom. "It's because we're special," said one of the seniors happily. "It's because Jennie's along," said Amanda cynically.

I was not surprised to be sitting alone, but nothing is so lonely as sitting by yourself in a double seat. Having me along had a curious effect on the seniors. They lost their nervousness. After all, they had already lost to me, so there was no test anxiety. They would actually do *better* on the examination, because they weren't frightened.

"Maybe she won't win," said somebody.

"Jennie not win?" cried Amanda. "Unthinkable! Of course Jennie will win. Has Westerly ever had a star to compare with Jennie Quint?"

The bus turned off the exit and entered Hartford. It stopped at the edge of a small grubby park near an abandoned building. A stray cat stood in high brown winter weeds, frozen as if it had died standing up. I gasped in horror, and then realized the cat was perfectly alive, it was stalking some little creature I hadn't seen. The cat pounced, and swung a tiny rodent in the air.

I was inside that little mouse. I was being swung around, cruel teeth caught in my skin.

We drove on to the Sheraton. I had no roommate. There was an uneven number going, and nobody wanted to room with me. I had plenty of money, in case I wanted to go shopping, but nobody to shop with. We checked in our bags but we didn't get to see our rooms because we had to head straight for the government building where we'd take the exam. Dozens of teenagers were arriving at the same time. They didn't look like a particularly successful crowd. They just looked like kids.

I had to beat all but nineteen of them.

Most of them weren't looking at anybody. Maybe it's hard to stare in the eye the very people you plan to whip.

Or maybe I was the only one who planned to do that. Maybe only *my* parents at breakfast that morning had said, "We're counting on you, Jennie. You can do it. You always have, you always will. This is what we brought you up to do. *Succeed.*"

It was the "always" that kept ringing in my ears.

You ALWAYS have, you ALWAYS will.

ALWAYS, ALWAYS, ALWAYS.

And then I saw it in two words: all ways, Jennie Quint, you will succeed in all ways.

I could see my whole life out there—decades of it, millions of minutes of it—and always, always, in all ways, all ways, I had to succeed.

It made me dizzy.

Once you decide to do your best, you know where you'll be every minute: practicing, studying, working, struggling, or performing.

And will you do that alone?

Will I always, all ways, have no friends?

Will anybody take Emily's place, or Hillary's, or Paul's?

Dizzy.

I have to get a grip on myself.

The proctor is going to think my diary is a cheat sheet.

Put it under the chair.

You can't solve anything by writing it down, anyway.

Look at this examination. Does it solve anything? No. It adds to the problem. You have to win, Jennie, always, all ways, set the diary down and win.

I opened the third booklet of the day's torture and read the first page of math problems and knew I could not do them. The dizziness crawled over me until I had to hang onto the desk itself. I turned through the four pages of problems in the tiny awful pamphlet. I'd be able to get half.

Half! A grade of 50! I have to get over 90! I have to! I've got to win this!

The whole school is pitted against me! I can't go back and admit they're right, that I can't do it! I can't face that! I can't let Amanda win! I've got to be the junior they think I am! I have to win. I have to win. I have to win. I have to win.

The words pounded in my skull.

Thick vicious rhythm.

I have to win!

I have to win!

I always have to win!

The room was very large, and the desks widely spaced. A proctor stood at the front. The proctor had a paperback book she was reading, its cover folded so you couldn't tell if she was reading a mystery or a piece of meaningful, important twentieth-century literature.

Winning is what I do, I am a winner!

I chewed my hair, which I never do, and bit down on my pencil.

My parents brought up a winner, and I am a winner.

And glancing slightly ahead and to the left, I realized that Amanda was left-handed, and no blocking arm curled up to hide Amanda's paper. Big fat numerals paraded across Amanda's page. Amanda had the same problems to work that I did.

But she didn't have the same answers.

Amanda's answers would be right.

I sat in my seat, failing the math section of the test, and thought, *Oh, thank God! I can win after all! I just have to cheat!*

Emily's diary

Hillary and Jared and Ansley and Paul and I got called down to Dr. Sykes's office. In some ways I suppose we are a sort of group, but not really. Paul is all by himself, and Hill and I stick together, and Jared and Ansley are practically taped together—and yet, we are a crowd. But I could not imagine why Dr. Sykes wanted us.

And I don't think he could imagine why, either.

He was truly peculiar, asking truly peculiar questions, all centering on Jennie.

Paul Classified said, "But Dr. Sykes, she just got on the bus for Hartford yesterday morning. Isn't she taking the examinations with the seniors?"

Dr. Sykes said, "Uh, no. No, she—she isn't, Paul."

We stared at him. She had certainly gotten on the bus. We all saw her.

Dr. Sykes said, "During the third examination, she walked out of the room. It's not allowed and the proctor called to her to come back, but she didn't. That was yesterday. Nobody has seen her since."

Talk about stunned.

Hillary and I stared at each other. The Jennie we knew would never do a thing like that. Never!

Paul said, "She hasn't called us."

Now we stared at *him*. "Us?" repeated Hillary.

Jared said, as if it hardly mattered and we should have known this anyway, "Paul's living at our house now.

137

Dr. Sykes, do they think something happened to her? Or do they think she—uh—ran away?"

It was almost impossible to say the words. Jennie Quint—running away? Runaways are skanks on drugs, or kids whose parents abuse them, or nasty little creeps with nothing going for them who hate school anyhow. Jennie Quint, a runaway?

And yet, when you say, "Did something happen to her?" what do you mean? Kidnapping? Murder? Suicide?

Hillary has not been interested in Jennie for a long time. She said, "You're living with the Lowes, Paul? When did that happen?"

"Little while ago," said Paul irritably. I, who watch Paul ceaselessly, had not even seen that he has new clothes: a shirt that fits, sneakers first-day white, and a sweater that doesn't threaten to rip apart over his broad shoulders. "Dr. Sykes, what are they doing to find Jennie?" he asked, never glancing at Hillary.

Dr. Sykes stretched his hands out helplessly. "Not much. They don't have a clue. She's just gone. They have a photograph of her they showed at the airport, Amtrak, the bus station, and the rental car agencies, but the amazing thing is, in a snapshot, Jennie is pretty ordinary: brown hair, brown eyes, nobody can remember a thing."

"I don't think that's so amazing," muttered Hillary.

Paul said, "Maybe she's still in Hartford. Are they checking hotels? The Y? Does she have relatives up that way?"

Ansley said, "Well, Jennie simply would not jeopardize a test, so she must have absolutely had to go to the girls' room."

Dr. Sykes said, "Yes, but she would have come back from the girls' room, Ansley."

"Maybe somebody kidnapped her."

And Paul Classified said in the queerest, saddest voice, "No. Kidnapping doesn't really happen. They go because they want to."

Candy, I thought. He means Candy. Oh, Paul! I didn't even think, because I was so amazed about Jennie! Paul, it worked! My letter to Mr. Lowe worked! I knew he could help you!

I was so happy and pleased with myself I had to hide my joy: in this awful, mean year, I had done a good deed. Paul would never know, I would never tell anybody, not even Mr. Lowe. I put my hand over my mouth to cover up my expression.

"What can we do to help find Jennie, Dr. Sykes?"

It came from me at the same time it came from Paul. It was synchronized. Paul gave me a tight look that was sort of a smile but really a frown. The Lowes would get to know him: Ansley and Jared would get to know him. But not me.

And Dr. Sykes shrugged. Because nobody knew how to find Jennie.

JARED'S DIARY

Even gone, Jennie is a smash hit. Nobody in school is talking about anything except Jennie's disappearance.

I remember when I started this journal I had categories. That lasted about a week. Now the school has divided into categories over Jennie.

There's your violence crowd: they believe Jennie was

kidnapped or lured into prostitution and any day now her body will be found in the gutter. Half of me truly laughs at all that melodrama, and the other half of me can't eat lunch thinking about it.

There's your whose fault is this, anyway? crowd: they're blaming Jennie's parents for pushing her, and Amanda's crowd for yelling at her, and Emily and Hillary for abandoning her. Emily was crying all day. We all kind of gathered around. We couldn't be a team for Jennie now, but at least we could hand Emily another Kleenex. (Actually, I couldn't, I hate tissues, but Ansley really got into the image of herself as comforter.)

And then there's the Shrink of the Day crowd, analyzing Jennie's psyche. When she got to the math section, she couldn't take failure, they've decided. Her strength made her weak. (Whatever that means.)

But Paul Classified asked me if I thought Jennie would kill herself.

Since Paul does not joke, and does not exaggerate, and seems to have more experience with this kind of thing than I do, it really shook me up. "Jennie?" I said.

Ansley made me cut classes and hold her hand. There's nobody more self-sufficient than Ansley. But she kept saying, "What if Jennie is in trouble, Jared?"

"Obviously Jennie *is* in trouble."

"Oh, Jared, don't be a toad. What if it's bad and she's hurt and she needs us?"

I kept heaving these huge sighs. "Ansley, you and I are the last people Jennie Quint would call."

Ansley began weeping all over my shoulder. "Not the last!" she protested. "Amanda Hodges is the last."

"Ansley, have faith in Jennie. She's just too tough and too smart to get into that much trouble."

"But Jared, Jared, the things people were guessing at

in school—like what happened to that little boy Adam in Florida—murdered and cut in pieces." I tried to calm Ansley down. "Jennie's got her own credit card and some cash. She can charge till she reaches whatever limit she's got on it."

"If she's alive to sign the charges," said Ansley. "If nobody else is using the card."

So we drove on home because school stopped being school and turned into a guessing game about what horrible things could have happened to Jennie Quint.

And in my living room, where nothing more interesting than changing the wallpaper has ever taken place, there was Ansley counting on me to save Jennie from death, and Paul counting on my father to take him to visit his mother at the mental hospital, and Mrs. Quint getting consoled by my mother!

One month ago, we were building an addition and heading for a ski vacation. Now we're shoring up everybody in Westerly with emotional problems.

"You are *too* a fine parent," said my mother, handing Mrs. Quint a cup of tea. "These things happen to all of us," my mother added, trying to sound comforting.

We all stared at my mother. I in particular resented the implication that these things happen even in the Lowe family. My mother looked at me helplessly. I guess she can't say to Mrs. Quint, "You're a rotten parent and you should have expected this."

Ansley said, "Let's all go visit Mrs. Smith."

And Paul? Does he yell at her? Does he say this is classified? Does he try to strangle her? No. He smiles and says he would like that.

And to think a year ago I thought life was simple.

Emily's diary

The police were here.

Looking for information about Jennie.

They were nice-looking men: kind of huggy, actually, like big blue teddy bears. I was very surprised. The kind of person who would be at a crossing at an elementary school, not tracking drug runners or murderers. "You're Jennie's best friend, we understand?" they started.

I started to cry.

I am ashamed of those tears, because they weren't for Jennie. They were for me. If I'm a best friend . . .

They wanted to know if I thought Jennie had run away—or been taken. I said I didn't know. I said I really didn't have a single clue to where she would go if she were running away. And I don't. But I lay awake all night wondering.

Two in the morning. Three. Whispering, "Jennie, I'm sorry."

Toward dawn I said into the silent darkness, "Jennie, if you need me, you can call me. I'm still your friend. I promise."

But there is no evidence to support that.

So I doubt if she heard.

Hillary Lang, her journal

I said to the police, "She probably ran away."

Mrs. Quint had obviously been weeping for hours. "No! Why would she do that? She has everything! And the very finest of friends! She doesn't do things like that! She doesn't hang out or have bad acquaintances! Not my Jennie!"

Mrs. Quint lords it over everybody on Lost Pond Lane. She hasn't talked about basic things like weather or flowers or the Women's Club for ages; it's been Jennie this, Jennie that. And my poor mother always has to say weakly, "Well, our Hillary is happy." You can tell Mrs. Quint is glad there are losers like me to sit in Jennie's audience. My mother has never thrown china at Mrs. Quint or anything, which I think shows admirable restraint.

I said to the police, "She ran away. She'll do anything for attention."

Ansley's diary

So at last we know it all.

Paul was five when his little sister Candy was born.

His mother didn't want another child, didn't want Paul for that matter, was rough with them. Paul didn't say it, but I guess she really slapped him around, and the baby, too. And then she just left. Disappeared. Who could walk away from a newborn baby and a little boy starting kindergarten? I can't even imagine doing that. Wouldn't you lie awake your whole life long wondering if that baby was warm and fed and laughing? Wondering if your little boy was happy in school and joined the Cub Scouts and fell off his bike?

Anyway, Paul's father married again, and this second wife brought them up. Paul really loved her, and she's the one Paul calls Mom, and she's the only mother that Candy ever knew.

Okay, typical suburban story so far. And what happens last year? The real mother shows up and wants her kids back. She says she has a prior claim as the biological mother. And Candy says to the biological mother, "I've always known you would come for me one day! I want to live with you!" And off goes Candy, thrilled and happy, without a backward look. Paul's mom almost collapses— these are *her* kids. So when she starts falling apart the father can't take the pressure, and what happens? The father walks. Leaves.

Can you imagine?

What a bunch. Reliability first, you know?

Paul's mom has a total breakdown, as who wouldn't, thrown aside by the daughter she brought up and the man she loves? Paul's mom lives in constant fear that Paul won't come home one day because he doesn't really love her, either.

I said, "What about therapy?"

"Talking is nice, I suppose, although I don't do much of it myself, but talking doesn't change things. My mother is terrified, and I don't blame her. She can't trust anyone, including me, and I don't blame her. She feels worthless and no good, and I don't blame her."

Ah, dear diary.

You know what I have learned this year?

I have learned that I am lucky, lucky, lucky, lucky.

My family loves me. Nobody has abandoned me, nobody's going to. I have friends and relatives and roots and money. Luck of the draw, I guess. Poor Paul, poor Paul. What's classified is pain.

. . . . I stopped writing because I felt done.

I forgot about Jennie.

Am I really a person so shallow that all this is a soap opera to me, and I'm just watching other people's suffering like entertainment?

JARED'S DIARY

So after we talked about P.C.'s whole life—which was as depressing a story as I ever heard—no wonder he won't talk about it—we talked about Jennie. And where she could be, and why she did it. Paul didn't run off when he had problems big enough to drown in, so why did Jennie run off? I have thought and thought about what the kids are saying in school and I can't quite agree with it. But I haven't come up with anything better.

We were all sitting in the addition: great glass walls that look down the sloping grass and past the gardens into the marsh. It was dark, and the lights of the town lay far

away, and the stars above were lost in a storm that would
come during the night. My mother had fallen asleep on
my father's shoulder. My father has been home so much
lately. I guess he decided that with families and kids
collapsing left and right he should have better attendance.

Ansley said, "I think . . . maybe . . . it's because . . .
somebody needed Paul." She looked very intently out at
the almost invisible yard, gathering an almost invisible
answer. "Somebody couldn't live without Paul." Ansley
turned and looked at me, but her hair was in her eyes and
for once she didn't toss it back. She whispered, "Nobody
really needs Jennie."

"Her parents," my father said.

Ansley sniffed. She doesn't like the Quints. "Her parents just need something to show off. They could do as
well with a new Jaguar."

Hillary Lang, her journal

I wonder how she'll come back. It isn't easy, coming
back. You have to admit you're a jerk. I don't know why
they're all so worried about her. I have known Jennie
Quint very, very well for my whole life and there is
nothing Jennie can't do.

Paul is living with the Lowes. It's nice, because we
see him every day now. He's much friendlier. Mr. Lowe
spends a lot of time with Paul. If I was jealous of Jennie,
you would certainly think Jared would be jealous of Paul.
But he isn't.

Everybody's scared for her. They think that coming back will be so hard that she just won't come back. That no matter how bad it is "out there," Jennie will stay and suffer rather than come back humiliated and dumb. I have faith in Jennie's conceit—she doesn't really want anything to happen to the great Jennie Quint.

None of the seniors won Star Student anyhow; it went to the same high schools it always goes to. We must have bad breath or something.

Jennie's diary

Every time the bus stops I look out the window.
I think—I could get off here.
But I'm afraid to get off the bus.
If I get off the bus, I have to start living again.

Emily's diary

I think about Jennie every minute.
I think about such ordinary things. I took a shower this morning and used almond soap, which I love, and Jhirmak shampoo, and after I stepped out onto the thick soft vanilla colored mat, I dusted myself with Anais Anais

powder. I blew my hair dry until it felt the way the powder smelled: cloudy and pretty.

Her father thinks Jennie may have had a hundred dollars cash. It has to be gone by now. So what is Jennie using for soap and toothpaste? Where is Jennie sleeping? What is Jennie eating? When it's dark, on this February night, and icy cold, and snowing, where will Jennie be?

Downstairs my mother was yelling good-bye because she had to leave for work. I raced down with just my towel on to kiss her good-bye, and I said, "While you're in New York, keep an eye out for Jennie."

My mother sighed. "I don't envy the Quints. I went over to see them last night, and they have just about collapsed. You know, their whole lives were wrapped up in that girl. And this is how she repays them! By slapping them in the face."

I'm always surprised by the parents' point of view. I guess Jennie did slap them in the face—but oh, how we slapped her first! Especially me.

"Mom, it's been six days. How is she keeping her hair clean, do you suppose? Jennie always liked to wash her hair every other night."

"You just have to hope she'll come to her senses," said my mother, dashing out the door. It was sleeting. But maybe Jennie had taken a bus to Florida. Or California. Maybe she was already waitressing in Miami. Oh, Jennie, don't throw away all that you are! All that you could be!

Come to your senses, Jennie!

It's like calling a duck, you know? Here, duck, duck, duck, duck! I have some stale bread for you! Come to your bread!

Here, Jennie, Jennie, Jennie! Come to your senses!

Jennie's diary

It's my parents' fault! If Daddy hadn't given me a credit card I wouldn't have been able to buy these tickets. If they hadn't pushed me and pushed me, I wouldn't have been so super. I would have been ordinary and people would have liked me. Well, I'm ordinary now.

This is the real me. Your basic, no-frills Jennie.

And who is she?

She's a plain, brown-haired teenager nobody has noticed. Nobody has spoken to. Nobody has questioned.

She's a jerk.

She did a dumb, dumb, dumb thing. Anybody else would just have heaved a big sigh and failed the math section. But no, Jennie Quint, who has to do everything too much, too much—Jennie Quint left the state.

Why didn't I just sit there and fail? Why did I run out of the test room, and out of the building, and down the street? Why did the bus station have to be so close? Why did I have to see the sign? Why did that fat lady standing in line have to buy a ticket to Pittsburgh? Why did I buy a ticket, too?

It's Emily's fault. And Hillary's. They didn't have to be so mean to me! If I had friends this year, I wouldn't have done these dumb things! I wouldn't be sitting on this bus, with other people's radios playing, and other people's smelly bag lunches, and other people's laughter, and other people's destinations!

Paul's diary

Classified.

I used to love that nickname. Made it so much easier to hide.

Now I think I was dumb.

You keep secrets from everybody else, you end up keeping them from yourself, too. A person can't be classified. And you need help one day, you don't know how to get it, because you've never done any talking. I'm not crazy about Jared. But his father and mother are pretty terrific.

Phys. ed. coach talked to me again about sports.

I might.

Not this year, can't be after school for practice this year. But I might next year. He's all tense. Seniors can't be on junior varsity, he says, you've got to be good enough for varsity, you've got to start this year.

I might.

I just might.

There's no news on Jennie. I was over at her house this afternoon with Mrs. Lowe, who brought a casserole over to the Quints. She said she felt very dumb, taking broccoli and cheese instead of their daughter, but it would show that she cared. What an unbelievable house. It is truly perfect, like a glossy magazine, and afterward I said to Mrs. Lowe, "Were they training Jennie to be a prop?"

Mrs. Lowe said, "Oh, you children! You're so cruel! They were doing the best they could. They love Jennie."

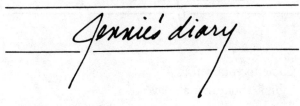

I didn't quite do it.

At least I can write that down, and it's true, it's not a lie.

I didn't actually cheat.

I only wanted to.

I thought of cheating as this wonderful, splendid, beautiful solution! It was waiting for me—crying, *You too can cheat and be a winner still!*

I set my pencil down very carefully.

Waited for the examination hour to end.

It was the longest and the shortest hour of my life.

Like waiting for my execution.

Failure.

It was there, in my hands: I had finally achieved failure.

Go home now?

Face my mother and father?

Say to them: I failed, do you still love me? Am I still a good enough trophy?

Right now there's only one thing to be proud of.

I didn't cheat.

Emily's diary

Come to your senses.

I think about that all day now.

Because what are the senses Jennie's supposed to come to?

Does it make sense to try so hard? To do so much? To be so shiny?

Does it make sense to lose your friends and your family?

But does it make sense just to hang around and not use your brain and your music?

Nothing makes sense. All of us being jealous doesn't make sense and Jennie's running away doesn't make sense. Sometimes now I think maybe something happened to her—she was kidnapped or killed or something—because it does not make sense, and everything Jennie did added up to a success, and this doesn't.

Jennie, Jennie, I'm sorry.

I've come to my senses, at least.

Please come to yours.

Jennie's diary

I got off the bus all of a sudden, thinking of Jared following Paul, thinking of police following me, thinking of being caught, like an animal, being caged, being yelled at, being bad, being wrong, being worthless.

I don't even know where it was, but it was a dark and horrible town.

I stood alone on the sidewalk and the bus pulled away. I ate a cheese sandwich from a vending machine and it was dry and I choked on it. I had a soda and when I used the bathroom behind the magazine counter, it was dirty and there were no paper towels.

I bought a magazine but I couldn't seem to read.

The music from the sonnet to snow blurred in my head and little bits of it played over and over and over and over again until I wanted to scream and rip my hair out and never hear the notes again.

I ran outside and ran down the street and I didn't stop until I had a pain in my side.

Leaves whipped by the winter wind rushed around my ankles, like little sheep wanting a shepherd. As if they wanted to be raked up and put in a cozy pile somewhere. If I had a match I would do it for them. I would set fire to them and they would be happy.

I walked through the icy dark past a bar where no commuter to New York would ever hang out. Garbage filled the gutters. A little girl came out of a side street, carrying a cardboard bucket of Kentucky Fried Chicken and a Pepsi. Her thin windbreaker was unzipped, and she had no hat, no scarf, and no mittens. The jacket was unzipped because the zipper was half torn off, hanging by its thin ribbon and waving in the wind. The only warm thing about her was the bucket, which steamed slightly around the edges.

I unzipped my thick luxurious ski jacket, took off my mittens, stuffed my scarf into the bookbag that swung from my bare fingers. Ye season, it was winter. Thirteen degrees, in a harsh wind. My fingers turned blue.

A car pulled up next to me.

A man leaned over the passenger side, from the driver's seat, and said something. His greasy hair was tied back under a bandanna that circled his forehead; a cigarette hung from the corner of his mouth, and filth rimmed the fingernails that gripped the opened window—a window that was always open: it was broken. His voice came through little shards of glass that poked up out of the opening.

I began running.

He simply drove alongside.

I ran faster.

He laughed, and stayed with me.

We came to an intersection and the cross street was one way: I raced the wrong direction up it so he could not follow. His laughter followed. Sick and depraved, it rang in my ears.

I found the bus station again, running the whole time, praying the car would not find me. I spent the night sitting on a wooden bench watching the minute hand on the wall clock go around. There wasn't much heat. A bus came around four in the morning and I got on.

Paul's diary

Came "home" today before Jared—he's in the drama production and had a rehearsal. I felt so strange walking in the front door of the Lowes' house. Mrs. Lowe was home, and we sat watching a soap opera. She loves the same soap opera Mom did, and has the same favorite character she worries about.

Mrs. Lowe said, "Shall I go with you to visit your mother?"

The visit was easy. Mrs. Lowe made it like a tea party, or something, so that we actually laughed. I didn't know Mom would ever laugh again. I didn't know I would ever laugh again. Coming home, Mrs. Lowe said, "Your biggest problem isn't going to be your mother, Paul."

I did laugh then. "Mrs. Lowe, if I have a larger problem out there than her, I don't even want to think about it."

She smiled. She said, "Forgiving Candy is going to be harder. Candy left without a backward look. Candy doesn't even notice what she did. Candy is genuinely happy with her biological mother. The eleven years your Mom spent bringing Candy up are gone as if they had never been, and Candy doesn't care. She's still your sister, she will always be your sister, and you hate her. That's what you have to get over, Paul. That's what's classified inside you."

Jennie's diary

I can't use my charge any more. They called my number in to the computer and I've reached my limit. Oh, how true, how true! I'm on my last ticket right now. I don't even know where this bus is going to end up. All I know is, I will have to get off.

I have a good coat, my scarf and gloves, my purse with six dollars left, my diary, three magazines, and half a bag of potato chips my last seatmate left. For lunch I had a candy bar and water from the drinking fountain at a station where we had fifteen minutes.

I don't look out the window. Ever. I look into myself.

I don't see good things.

What is the point in being born good if you hate yourself?

Paul's diary

She's right. I hate my sister.
I forgive my biological mother for coming back and

wanting us again, even though we didn't hear from her for ten years. I forgive Dad for not being able to stand the stress of his first wife taking his child away from his second wife, and vanishing. I forgive Mom for collapsing. I forgive Mom for caring more that Candy left than that I stayed.

But I can't forgive Candy.

I hate her.

Admitting it is half the battle.

It's not classified now, even to me.

And so I feel better toward Candy.

I still haven't said "thank you" to anybody. I thanked Mr. Lowe for the clothes. I thanked Mrs. Lowe for dinner. I haven't thanked Emily. I haven't thanked Jared for taking me in as if he liked me. I haven't thanked Ansley for going to visit my mother, too.

And I haven't thanked Jennie.

I learned something from Jennie. Never be jealous. Never believe that somebody else's life is perfect.

At lunch on Saturday I said to Mrs. Lowe, "Do you think Jennie is all right?"

"A girl without money has to figure out some way to eat, Paul. I tremble when I think what she might decide to do."

Jennie's diary

I changed buses. The bus driver was starting to talk to me. He knows I've run away from home. He told me

Greyhound gives free rides home to runaways. He would arrange a free ride home.

A free ride.

My whole life has been a free ride.

That's what happens when you're smart and talented: you go everywhere for free. But I don't want to anymore! I want to be just like everybody else, and fail some and be ordinary some, and be okay some. I don't want to shine all alone!

The Awesome Threesome.

We weren't awesome one by one.

We were awesome because we had two to share with.

The bus driver said, "You could share a few things with me, kid. Like your name and your parents' phone number."

So I got off the bus. I sat half the night in the station until another bus came. I cried the whole time.

Hillary Lang, her journal

We've talked so much about Jennie lately. My mother said we all have to forgive Jennie for having everything.

My father said if Jennie really and truly had everything, she wouldn't have run away, and it just goes to show you a family can look all shiny and perfect on the outside and be rotten on the inside. He said nobody runs away from a nice family.

For a minute I felt good, saying out loud the Quints aren't nice.

But then I remembered all of it: every tuna-fish sandwich Mrs. Quint made for us, every trip to the beach, every Band-Aid she put on my knee because I was always the one who fell down.

I've never liked Mrs. Quint. And after all these years, I still hardly know Mr. Quint. But I could at least go over there and tell her I'm sorry it all happened to them.

My father said, "Well, I'm sure I'm the crummiest person around, but I for one am glad that the Quints finally fell down in public."

"You're not the crummiest one, Dad," I told him. "The whole school said that the first day."

"And what did they say the second day?" Dad wanted to know. "And the third, and fourth, and fifth?"

Jennie's diary

Suppose I went home and was nothing.
Just me: a girl with brown hair.
Would they still love me?
They can't frame what I am today in this bus station.
I don't even know what town it is.
I don't even care.

JARED'S DIARY

I lie awake at night sometimes and wonder where Jennie's living.

Hey! Star of the East, come back!

All those places where you should be shining—you're not!

All those things you could be starring in—you're not!

As for Paul, I'm glad this house has lots of bedrooms and bathrooms. He's a very polite guest, but he and my mother are endlessly Questing for Answers: talking Life, and Truth, and Morality. If I say something like, "So— what's for supper, Mom?" they both look at me as if I'm their local resident mental defective. Twice I have gotten supper for them, and they took this meal as if they deserved it, and Mom even said it was good for me to be the servant for a change.

Paul's servant.

I do not care for this change of events.

However, the other night Ansley was here, and Hillary and Emily came over because they were depressed about Jennie, and we all played Monopoly half the night, and Paul actually laughed. Out loud and everything. Ansley congratulated him and made up a little Laugh Chart. She says every time he laughs she'll give him a gold star. That made him laugh, too, so she licked a little gold star we found in the back of the crayon box my mother's had since I was a little kid, and she pasted it on his forehead.

For a minute I got jealous of Paul, because Ansley's never pasted a gold star on my forehead, but Ansley kissed me good night later, when I took her home, and she said, "But Jared, darling, you are just one solid spectacular gold star." So I decided not to be jealous of Paul Classified.

Jennie's diary

I could call home.
I have a Calling Card.
But they'll yell at me.
Because they're going to feel responsible. They're going to be failures. They were parents who didn't do it right after all, just when they thought they were perfect.
They only loved me because I was perfect.
I was the trophy on their wall.
They won't love me now that I've ruined it.
So I can't call home.
Who could I call?
Not Emily, not Hill, not Paul, not their parents, not Miss Clinton, not anybody I can think of.
I'm sitting here in this bus station and now, at last, I am alone.
I only thought I was alone before.
Now it's real.

Paul's diary

I said, "What do you think made her run away, Mr. Lowe?" I asked him because I had this sense that he had all the answers to everything. He laughed. "I haven't had a conversation with Jennie in years," he told me, "but if I had to guess I'd say that endless perfection and achievement can be as horrible for a person as endless failure and pain."

"That's ridiculous," said Jared, just before I did.

First time I ever had anything in common with Mr. Preppy Jared.

Jennie's diary

So here I am.

A bus station far away.

Twinkies for dinner and dirty hair.

So far I have blamed

    a) my parents, for pushing me

    b) Hillary and Emily, for abandoning me

    c) Paul, for not loving me back

d) fate, for making me different

e) my parents, for giving me money

Jennie Dunstan Quint, I think it's time to xxxx out those and put in the real one. You. (Like at basketball games, when somebody fouls, and everybody in the bleachers stands up and points and shouts "YOU YOU YOU YOU YOU!")

You could have gone to the English teacher and told her not to post your papers. You could have gone to the home-ec department and asked if the classes there could help with the costumes. You could have asked Emily to be your partner in the laser experiment so she wouldn't have to do boring library research and you'd have a friend for a term paper. You could have told your mother to stop boasting to the neighbors and you . . .

Or maybe not.

Maybe no matter what you did, you would be isolated.

Maybe that's what success has to be.

Isolation.

I've started laughing.

Because sitting on that last bus, driving into the snow, realizing that I've made almost a complete circle and this bus is going to stop only two hundred miles from home—another song came to me. "Ye Season, It Was Winter." I can see the ice storm, and the burials, and the fear: I can hear percussion making the sounds of branches rubbing eerily and ice snapping under boots; I can hear an English horn weeping for a child . . . I am ready to compose the rest of my next musical.

I am ready to tell my mother I'm sorry.

I am ready to tell my father I'm sorry.

I am ready to face the whole school, and admit I'm a jerk, and shrug, and ask if anybody wants to help on next fall's musical.

I'm ready to be me.

Emily's diary

She called me.

She called *me*!

Out of all the people in this world who were scared for her, and wanted her home, and yearned to help—she called me.

"I'm coming," I said.

I didn't know how. I don't have a car or a license. And then Jennie said, "I've sat here so long, Em, it doesn't matter how long it takes you to get here. I'll just wait."

I set the phone down. And you know what? I began talking to God instead of Jennie, crying, "Thank you, God!"

I guess for another chance—I guess because Jennie forgave me for all my meanness—I guess because after all this terrible year—*I am the one who is a success.* For Paul and now for Jennie, I am the one who saved them.

So success isn't writing musicals, or getting A plus, or being interviewed in the newspaper.

Success is being proud of yourself.

That's why I hated Jennie. I wasn't proud of myself. But now I can help her, now I am stronger, now I can let go of that terrible jealousy and just be her friend.

Of course, I don't have a car to get her in, and I promised not to tell my parents or hers, and she thinks— and she's right—that Hillary is still as jealous as ever—so that leaves . . . who?

Paul's diary

I never had a stranger ride.

Emily came over at eleven o'clock at night.

Jared and Ansley had just gotten in from a date and we were watching a movie before Jared took Ansley on home, and Emily walks right in, takes a handful of popcorn, and says with her mouth full, "Jennie just telephoned me. We have to go get her. She's in Albany. It's a four-hour drive."

"Why did you have popcorn before you told us?" demanded Ansley.

"Because I'm nervous. I always eat when I'm nervous."

Jared leaped up, whooping and hollering. He did an Indian war dance around the room and yelled, "I love it! My life is perfect! I've always wanted to drive off in the middle of the night, a knight in shining armor, and rescue somebody. A four-hour drive! I love it. Maybe it'll snow! Maybe we'll have a hard time getting there! Maybe we'll get hijacked!"

"Nobody hijacks cars, Jared."

"A person can always dream." Jared laughed and told us how we would all squash into his Porsche and be a party of White Knights in Shining Armor, racing up to the bus station!

"Good thing it's a Friday and everybody's parents are out," said Jared happily. "Otherwise they'd ruin this by going themselves, or telephoning the police in Albany to get her. Oh, this is wonderful! Ansley, get everything in the refrigerator so we'll have plenty to eat. Emily, choose some good tapes for the drive! Paul, add up everybody's cash. We need money."

I collected wallets and purses and threw it all in a pile.

And I began laughing with Jared.

It was pretty wonderful.

Jennie was okay—and I am too.

I made it. Everybody I know helped me, whether I wanted it or not. And Jennie, she'll make it too. And my mother: I think Mom is going to make it.

Some of the anger and jealousy and worry seeped out of me.

My laughter was real.

Life could begin again.

Unclassified.

Emily said dubiously, "I'm not sure we should make a party out of this. Do you think Jennie wants us to arrive celebrating, with Cokes and cassettes?"

Ansley said, "Darling, Jennie wants friends. Four is better than one."

Ansley's diary

She was all right. I knew she would be.

She was dirty and hungry, but she wasn't suicidal or anything.

We all hugged.

It was slow, and it was circular, first me hugging her, and then Jared (and we're the two who matter least of all), and then Paul Classified, and then, at last, Emily. And the hug with Emily—oh, the hug of a friend who forgives you and you forgive her—oh, that was a hug to see.

Emily's diary

Paul asked me out.
Paul asked me out.
Paul asked me out.
Paul asked me out!
Paul !!! asked !!! me!!! out!!!!!!!!!!!!!!!!!!!!!!!!!!!!!!!!!!!!
(He did. It's true.)

Paul's diary

I never thought I would do a normal thing like go out on a date with a girl. I thought I would spend the rest of my life trying to keep my mother afloat. Mr. Lowe said bit by bit being normal will come back to me and it won't really be that hard.

Emily was so pleased that I asked her. I didn't know

167

she would be that pleased. I thought she would say yes, or I wouldn't have asked her—but I didn't know she would get all happy and giggly and give me a hug.

I haven't had a hug in a long time. Friday night I hugged everyone I know.

It was pretty great.

I could get into that kind of thing.

Emily's diary

The journals were due today.

Miss MacBeth was late to class, and we all sat there, hugging our diaries. Afraid to let go of them.

Hillary tore half hers out. She doesn't think Miss MacBeth will notice but I know Miss MacBeth will. I bet she doesn't grade Hill down, though. She'll figure if the entries meant so much they had to be destroyed, then Hill's diary was the best of all.

Ansley asked who was going to keep on with a journal now that we don't have to. If anybody is, nobody admitted it.

Well, I'm going to keep a diary forever, and I'll never tell a soul. Not The Awesome Threesome, not my mother, not Miss MacBeth, not even Paul. This diary will be for me. I have a new stenography notebook clipped inside my American history three-ring notebook. I'm writing in it now, and nobody in this room has noticed. They're watching—who else?—Jennie.

Jennie doesn't have a diary to pass in. She lost it in

the bus station. "You're going to get a zero," Jared said to her.

Jennie shrugged. Imagine Jennie Quint shrugging. She said, "It's only a diary I lost. I found the things that count."

Emily's Diary Number Two.

May it contain the things that count.

About the Author

Caroline B. Cooney is the award-winning author of several novels for young adults, including *I'm Not Your Other Half* and *Don't Blame the Music*. She lives in Westbrook, Connecticut.